The
ESSENTIAL COLLECTION

The

ESSENTIAL COLLECTION

#1 *New York Times* **Bestselling Author**

DEBBIE MACOMBER

STARLIGHT

⊕ **HARLEQUIN**®
ESSENTIAL DEBBIE MACOMBER COLLECTION

Recycling programs
for this product may
not exist in your area.

ISBN-13: 978-0-373-47312-0

Starlight

Copyright © 1983 by Debbie Macomber

For questions and comments about the quality of this book, please contact us at CustomerService@Harlequin.com.

Printed in U.S.A.

DEBBIE MACOMBER

is a number one *New York Times* and *USA TODAY* best-selling author. Her books include *1225 Christmas Tree Lane*, *1105 Yakima Street*, *A Turn in the Road*, *Hannah's List* and *Debbie Macomber's Christmas Cookbook*, as well as *Twenty Wishes*, *Summer on Blossom Street* and *Call Me Mrs. Miracle*. She has become a leading voice in women's fiction worldwide and her work has appeared on every major bestseller list, including those of the *New York Times*, *USA TODAY*, *Publishers Weekly* and *Entertainment Weekly*. She is a multiple award winner, and won the 2005 Quill Award for Best Romance. There are more than one hundred million copies of her books in print. Two of her Harlequin MIRA Christmas titles have been made into Hallmark Channel Original Movies, and the Hallmark Channel has launched a series based on her bestselling Cedar Cove series. For more information on Debbie and her books, visit her website, www.debbiemacomber.com.

To my daughters Jody and Jenny,
who have always wanted me to name
characters after them.

One

Karen had dreaded the party for weeks. Her father was sure to use it as another opportunity to find her a husband. She almost cringed at the thought of what lay before her—a succession of eligible men, abrupt introductions, and pointed questions. Yet she loved her godparents and wouldn't offend them by not attending their annual Christmas party.

"Are you ready, lass?" Matthew McAlister let himself into her apartment without the courtesy of knocking.

"Honestly, Dad, one of these days you're going to walk in here and find me stark naked," Karen admonished with a sigh.

Matthew chuckled.

Karen laughed, too, for it was difficult to maintain an injured air when her father was in this mood.

Stepping back to survey Karen, Matthew's

eyes lit up in appreciation. "My heart swells with pride at the sight of you, lass," he said in a strong Scottish brogue.

Karen forced herself to smile. His speech always began the same way. After admiring her beauty, he would recount the days he'd courted her mother and their marriage when Madeline was nineteen. From there he'd reiterate his growing desire for grandchildren, most particularly a granddaughter. It was always the same, to the point that Karen could have mouthed the words along with him.

"Dad," she interrupted, "we'd better go. Snoqualmie Falls is a forty-five-minute drive."

Surprisingly, Matthew insisted Karen drive. She did so willingly, but glanced apprehensively at her father. He looked tired and a bit ashen.

"Are you feeling okay, Dad?" she asked, hiding the concern in her voice.

"Of course I am." He rallied somewhat. "I'm just saving myself for the grand affair. Certain demands are made of a widower these days, and the ladies are expecting a good time."

They were greeted at the large rented hall with soft Christmas music. The room was lavishly decorated with hundreds of large, glittering snowflakes suspended from the ceiling. The reflective glow of the turning flakes cast the dimly lit room into a winter wonderland.

The hall was already crowded. Several others had arrived and were milling around, chatting in small groups and sipping champagne.

Evan Forsyth raised a welcoming hand when he saw Matthew and Karen enter, and walked purposefully toward them. The two men clasped hands with the enthusiasm of many years of devoted friendship.

Her father and Evan had been friends since their school days, and although they held separate stations in life, their friendship had never wavered. Evan Forsyth was the president of the University of Washington at Tacoma, an honored and respected man, while Matthew McAlister was a small-businessman dealing in plumbing supplies. For as long as Karen could remember, her father and godfather had played chess every Thursday night.

The annual party had begun many years before, when Karen and her sister, Judy, were small. Evan and Milly Forsyth invited a few intimate friends into their home to share the joy of the holiday season. Over the years, as Evan's position became prominent, the size of the affair had grown to include business friends and faculty members. This year, the party was so large the Forsyths had rented a hall, their spacious home no longer large enough to hold the growing number of guests.

"Welcome, welcome," Evan said and smiled warmly. His wife, Milly, followed close behind and embraced Karen fondly.

"I'm so pleased you could make it, my dear."

Evan leisurely surveyed Karen, noting how the red velvet gown molded to the slender curves of her womanly figure.

"I swear you get prettier every year, Karen," he said with a hug.

"And I swear your tongue grows smoother every year."

Evan chuckled with delight while Milly tucked an arm around Karen's waist to give her a slight hug. "He's right, dear. You look radiant. And your gown suits you beautifully."

Karen returned the hug and smiled. "It should, considering what I paid for it."

Karen had gasped when the salesclerk had told her the price, and disregarded the woman's complimentary words as an effective sales pitch. But now she willingly conceded that the effect of the simple but elegant style had been worth the price.

The four chatted until social obligations demanded the Forsyths' attention. After sampling several of the hors d'oeuvres and speaking with acquaintances, Karen and her father watched as the floor was cleared to make room for dancing.

Matthew surveyed the crowd while gently directing Karen as they danced the first waltz. His eyes glowed with amusement as he remarked, "There are several available men here. Take advantage of the opportunity to snare yourself a husband."

Karen stiffened and pulled away from her father.

Almost angrily, Matthew continued, "I can't understand what's the matter with men today. You're lovely, Karen."

"Dad, please…" A note of helplessness entered her voice. Karen was so weary of this argument. A thousand times she'd explained that the problem wasn't with men; it was with her. So many of the men she'd dated over the years were self-centered and egotistical, seeking easy conquests and one-night stands. It was almost to the point that she'd rather not date at all. Her natural good looks and vivacious personality invited the attention. But Karen had yet to discover what it was about herself that attracted the least-desirable males.

"I'm perfectly content with my life as it is." Karen sighed with impatience, tilting her chin defiantly.

"But I want grandchildren…"

"You have grandchildren," Karen reminded him coolly. "What do you call James and Carter?"

"I want a granddaughter." Matthew flashed her a disputatious look.

"Dad," Karen pleaded, "let's not argue tonight. You have grandchildren, and more than likely you'll have your precious granddaughter." Karen didn't know how much more she could endure. Matthew had applied constant pressure on her to marry for the past six months. The argument had nearly ruined their close relationship. Unable to endure his interference with her life, Karen had moved into her own apartment. It was a move long overdue. It'd been convenient to live at home and easy to rationalize her father's need for her after her mother's death. Much to her chagrin, Matthew sold their home and moved into an apartment in the same building as Karen. If anything, matters had gotten worse.

As they continued to waltz across the room, Karen caught sight of Mabel Jackson, an aging widow who'd made no effort to disguise her attraction to Matthew. *Turnabout is fair play,* she mused, and giggled devilishly.

"Do you find something amusing, lass?" Matthew asked curiously.

"No. Excuse me, Dad. I see someone I'd like to talk to." Cleverly, she wove her way through the thick couples toward the widow.

"Mrs. Jackson, you look lovely tonight," Karen greeted sweetly.

Mabel Jackson ignored the greeting and craned her long neck to stare into the dancing figures.

"Is your father here?" she asked with obvious interest.

"He sure is. In fact, it was my father who commented on how radiant you look. Dad said he'd never seen anyone more lovely."

"He did?" The woman beamed and smoothed the hairs of her lopsided wig.

"You know, Mrs. Jackson, my father is a lonely man. He'd never admit it, of course, but Dad needs a woman. A real woman." Karen stared into the crowd, unable to meet the widow's triumphant gaze.

Mabel Jackson positively glowed. "My dear child, I'm so glad we've had this little talk. Leave your father to me."

Karen smiled broadly and felt that even if she ended up disinherited, the taste of revenge was indeed sweet.

In a matter of minutes, several men were vying for Karen's attention. She danced with a number of partners, young and old, her infectious laughter ringing through the hall as she surrendered to a swelling tide of triumph. Not once was she interrupted by her father's forcing what he considered eligible men on her. An hour later, she managed to catch Matthew's eye and winked wickedly as he waltzed by in the arms of Mabel Jackson. Matthew cast her a look that threatened bodily harm, and Karen burst into helpless giggles.

A moment later, she caught sight of her father's angry stride as he wove through the crowd toward her. Wishing to avoid the taste of his Scottish temper, she hastily sought an escape. A curtained glass door leading to a balcony caught her attention. Unnoticed, she quietly slipped into the dark, leaving her father perplexed by her sudden disappearance.

Peering through the sheer curtain, Karen waited impatiently for Matthew to abandon his search.

"I beg your pardon," came a deep voice from behind her as she backed into a solid form.

"Oh! Excuse me." She fumbled and quickly straightened. "I didn't realize there was anyone out here."

"Obviously," came the clipped reply as he stared into the dark. Karen watched him for a few minutes, but he made no effort to meet her gaze.

"Would you mind sharing your hideaway for a minute?" she asked sweetly, and deliberately blinked her long, curling lashes at his impassive expression. Men were usually quick to respond to her expressive brown eyes.

"Suit yourself," he retorted unenthusiastically, and continued to stare into the night.

Undaunted by his lack of welcome, Karen joined him at the railing and searched the sky to discover what was so fascinating. The night was cold, crisp, and clear; the stars shone with a brilliant intensity.

"Leave it to my godfather to order a star display for the night of his party," Karen murmured. Her gaze returned to the stranger's face and swept his appearance. He wore a trim-fitting, dark wool suit that hugged his slim hips and long legs. The harsh contours of his face remained blank under her examination.

"Look!" Karen exclaimed, pointing her finger to the sky and counting the stars. "It's Perseus. I can't remember when I've seen the constellation stand out so clearly. You do see it, don't you?"

"No, I'm afraid I don't," he remarked dryly.

"Sure you do. Just look a little to your left," she persisted.

"Listen," he snapped impatiently, "whatever your name may be—"

"Karen McAlister," she interrupted, "and you're...?"

"Randall Prescott," he replied in a voice that spoke plainly of trepidation.

"Well, look again. It's up there plain as day."
She pointed to it again for his benefit. "Really,
it's very clear, if you'll just look…"

"Mrs. McAlister…"

"Miss," Karen informed him cheerfully.

"Miss McAlister…" he tried again.

"Please call me Karen."

Drawing in a breath as if to hold on to his
limited patience, he began again. "Karen…Miss
McAlister…whatever it is you wish to be called,
I cannot view your precious Perseus, and I shall
never view it. I'm blind!"

Karen felt the full impact of shock. After a
moment of startled silence, she blurted out, "Oh,
dear, Mr. Prescott, I do apologize."

"Randall," he interrupted.

"I had no idea, Randall. I…"

"Please call me Rand," he taunted softly.

"All right, Rand," she replied, a smile evident
in her voice, "but please accept my apology."

"An apology is unnecessary; my blindness
cannot be attributed to your faults," he countered stiffly.

"No, of course not, but I was being obtuse."

He turned toward her then, allowing for the
first time a clear view of his rugged features.
He certainly didn't fit her image of what a blind
man might look like. His face was boldly defined, almost ruthless. There was a magnetic

quality about his dark brown eyes that captured her gaze.

"I don't suppose you came out here without your coat to view the stars?" he asked roughly, as if aware of her eyes studying him.

"How do you know I'm not wearing a coat?" she asked. Was this unnerving man playing her for a fool?

A sardonic smile touched the corners of his mouth. "I don't. But I suspect the slight quiver in your voice is from a chill."

Karen suddenly realized she was cold. Snoqualmie Falls was only a few minutes from the summit of Snoqualmie Pass, over the Cascades. The bitter December wind bit into her.

"Why are you hiding?" he asked, more gently. "Is someone bothering you?"

"Oh, heavens, no!" she quickly assured him, but paused. "Well, yes and no. I routed a persistent widow toward my father and was sure to taste his anger had I remained inside."

Rand smiled at her predicament, his roguish features relaxing his expression. "I'm sure the whole incident has been forgiven. You can't stay here. You'll freeze."

It was clearly a dismissal, and Karen felt strangely disappointed. She wanted to stay and learn more about this enigmatic stranger. He was the first man to really interest her in a long while. She hovered in the doorway, hoping to find an excuse to remain, but found none.

"Are you coming, too?"

"Later," he replied indifferently, and appeared bored with her company.

Karen could only leave. "Then perhaps we'll meet again," she said softly.

"It's unlikely," he mumbled, as if he hadn't intended her to hear. She watched as he returned to the railing.

Karen didn't immediately see her father once she'd entered the warmth of the large reception hall. Mrs. Jackson was standing near the orchestra, waving her hand impatiently in an attempt to gain the conductor's attention.

"Here you are."

The voice startled Karen, and she jerked around to see her godfather. "Uncle Evan." She placed a trembling hand over her heart to dramatize her fright. "You're worse than a thief in the night."

Evan Forsyth's eyes twinkled. "Your father's looking for you."

Karen lowered her gaze, a little ashamed of her ploy. As much as Matthew irritated her, she loved him and realized he had only her best interests at heart.

"I suppose he's still angry?" she asked.

"Let's put it this way," Evan said, chuckling.

"He hasn't had a free second since you spoke with Mabel. He's hiding in the men's room. I think we'd better dance before he decides it's safe to return."

"Oh, dear, I'm in for it now," she mumbled as her godfather led her to the dance floor. It was a waltz, which gave her the opportunity to speak. "I'm afraid I made a blunder with one of your guests."

Evan's eyes rounded, feigning shock. "You seem to be making a night of it, my dear. Want to talk about it?" His position with the university and in the community made him a ready listener to the troubles of others.

Karen felt uneasy. "I'm afraid I literally bumped into Randall Prescott—"

"Ah," Evan interrupted her. "I imagine he was rude. He tends to be the prickly sort. Damn good professor, though, the finest. We offer the best business program in the state due to him. Prescott could teach anywhere. The university is lucky to have him." He hesitated, his thick brows knitting his forehead. "Was Cora with him?"

"Cora? No. Who's she?" It hadn't occurred to Karen that Rand was married. The thought deflated her.

"That's unusual. Rand rarely attends any social functions without her."

"Is Cora his wife?" Karen hoped to hide any telltale inflection of curiosity from her voice.

"No, she's a business associate. They've collaborated together, books and the like."

Karen felt herself relax, an excitement flowing through her limbs.

Sensing her interest, Evan felt obliged to add, "I wouldn't discourage you, Karen, but Randall Prescott is a bit of a cynic. A difficult man to get to know. He's independent and proud, highly defensive of his blindness. He's not your normal chivalrous hero…tread carefully."

"Who says I'm interested?" Karen asked defensively.

Evan chuckled. "Karen, I've known you all your life. Certainly I know you well enough to recognize that gleam in your eye."

Several minutes later, Karen saw Rand sitting unobtrusively in the rear of the hall. She had been waiting for his appearance, silently searching faces. Now she wondered how to gain his attention. In answer to her problem, the orchestra conductor turned to face his audience and announced the first ladies' choice of the evening.

Mabel Jackson, with a satisfied smirk, made a beeline for Matthew, who had recently reappeared. Karen groaned in sympathy and walked toward the back of the reception room and the mystifying Randall Prescott.

Without introduction or preamble, she curtsied. "May I have the pleasure of this dance?"

Rand sat up abruptly and stiffened. "Miss McAlister?"

"Karen," she corrected impishly.

"All right, *Karen*. Let's not go through that again." A smile threatened the stiff line of his mouth.

He hesitated so long, Karen grew uncomfortable. "You did hear them mention it was ladies' choice, didn't you?"

He held his shoulders stiff and formal. "I'm honored, but no." His mouth remained inflexible.

Karen would have been surprised if he'd accepted. "Well, that's fine; my feet are beginning to ache, anyway. New shoes," she explained before taking the seat beside him.

If he was surprised, he didn't show it. "Have a seat," he offered sarcastically.

Karen ignored his derision. "Thank you, I have."

Apparently, he felt no inclination to speak, and Karen was courteous enough not to press. After a dance or two, she discovered that she was completely content to sit with him, not talking, if he wished. She hummed and watched the dancers as they waltzed through the wintry scene. She could almost see Rand relax his guard and accept her company.

"Aren't the decorations magnificent?" she asked thoughtlessly, then gasped, recognizing her blunder. How stupid could she be? "If my new shoes are tight, I needn't worry," she apologized. "After they've been in my mouth a couple of times, they'll fit fine. That was stupid. Please excuse me," she added soberly.

"Don't worry," he assured her, almost enjoying her discomfort. "It's a common mistake. Describe the decorations, will you?"

It was a pleasure to narrate the lovely scene portrayed by the dangling snowflakes. With her natural flair for theatrics, she described the hall in graphic detail. In afterthought, she added interesting tidbits she knew about some of its occupants.

"It's almost impossible to tell when Uncle Evan is angry or upset, but he has a telltale twitch in his upper lip. If you see it move, watch out. And then there's Clayton Dunbar, a distant relative of the Forsyths'. He's about as subtle as a garden serpent and has the sincerity of a used-car salesman. He marks his conquests on his bedpost to brag to his friends."

"Do I detect a note of mockery?"

"No use hiding the fact that I detest the man.

He's about as obvious as a Sherman tank." It was unlike Karen to be catty, and she immediately felt guilty. Besides, was she being any less obvious about her interest in Rand? "That's unfair. I'm sure Clayton has several good qualities…somewhere."

Rand gave a hearty laugh. "You're apt at describing others. How would you depict yourself?"

"I couldn't," she protested automatically. "How do you picture me?"

"You have an intriguing voice." He paused, thinking. "But I'm not referring to the tone quality. You possess an unshakable resolve. I doubt that you've ever failed in any pursuit. You're upbeat, cheerful."

"Heavens," Karen said dryly, "you make me sound like a high school cheerleader."

"Definitely not high school. You must be all of nineteen, maybe twenty."

Karen laughed lightly. "I'm a whole world away from high school or college. I'm twenty-three."

Rand grinned, then added, "You must be five-seven, five-eight at the most."

Impressed, Karen lifted her brows expressively. "Five-seven."

"Long dark hair and metallic-blue eyes."

"Short dark curls, equally dark eyes."

A hand cupped the back of her neck; his fingers twisted the pliable curls. Karen was too startled by the sudden action to protest. Her heart rate soared as a languorous warmth spread from her neck.

He chuckled softly and said, "Yes, short, but soft and inviting. Your eyes must be expressive, promising." He relaxed against his chair, the dim light illuminating his strongly defined features. Again, Karen experienced the full impact of his masculinity.

"That's not quite right, but I'm not going to disillusion you with the truth." She laughed because she'd always thought her dark eyes, the color of bitter chocolate, were plain. Rand made them sound exciting and enticing.

"Give me your hand," he said suddenly. When she complied, his fingers gently examined hers. "You're not a secretary, or your fingertips wouldn't be this smooth. Nor do you walk with the crisp purpose of a nurse."

"That's a chauvinistic attitude. All women aren't secretaries or nurses. I'm not a teacher, either."

"Aha!" He laughed again. "You're employed in a man's field."

Karen smiled at his novel methods of deducing her occupation, but the smile died quickly as she spied Clayton Dunbar eyeing her from the edge of the dance floor. She stiffened instinctively, her reluctance obvious.

"Is something wrong?" Rand questioned.

"My wicked past is about to catch up with me. Dad's revenge is here." Karen had dated Clayton only once and spent the entire evening fighting off his sexual advances. She hadn't told her father for fear of offending the Forsyths; now she recognized her error.

"Karen, baby, it's good to see you. I see you've been waiting for me. Let's dance."

Karen's mind whirled, searching for a plausible excuse to refuse as she stood.

Suddenly, Rand rose beside Karen, his imposing frame dwarfing Clayton's. "Excuse me," he said stiffly, "but you'll have to wait your turn. This dance is mine."

In his eagerness to corner Karen, Clayton hadn't noticed her formidable companion. His smug expression instantly turned to that of a deprived child.

Karen's mood lightened immediately. Placing her hand in Rand's, she led the way to the dance floor. With a devilish gleam, she turned back and smiled cheerfully. "Ta-ta, Clayton."

Rand took the lead, guiding her firmly but cautiously through the array of dancers. The dance floor was unfamiliar territory, but his movements were made skillfully and with confidence. He held her lightly, and a warmth flowed through her.

"How are we doing?" he questioned.

"Fine," she assured him. "You don't like to dance, do you?" He so obviously didn't, Karen wondered what had made him offer.

"Let's just say I have an easy enough time making a fool of myself without doing it purposely."

Impulsively, Karen raised her head and gently laid her lips against the rough line of his jaw. "Thank you," she whispered softly.

He drew her slightly closer, and her mind whirled in a confused mixture of emotions. Surely she hadn't imbibed that much champagne. A glass or two, three at the most. Why should this one man affect her like this?

"I didn't want to let you go," he whispered into her hair, as if admitting to a fault, his voice low and husky.

"I didn't want to go, either." She sighed and rested her head against the velvety texture of his suit jacket.

His fingers spread across the small of her back, molding her slender figure against him. The beat of his heart sounded in her ear, telling her he was as affected by their closeness as she. Slowly, his hand stroked the back of her neck, his fingers entwining with her hair.

It wasn't necessary to talk. Karen hummed the melody as the musicians played, but the tune was inaudible compared to the glorious song her heart was singing. Somehow she'd always known it would be like this. Matthew had claimed he met Madeline and decided to marry her all in the space of one day's time. Karen had secretly scoffed. Choosing a life partner wasn't something one did after only a few hours' acquaintance. Now Karen realized her father had spoken the truth. Just as he had known, she knew now. She didn't love Rand; not yet. That would come later. But Karen had never been more certain of anything in her life. It was crazy, unorthodox.

"You're smiling, aren't you?" Rand asked after some time.

Karen had a difficult time finding her voice or thinking coherently. When she did answer, her voice was weak and low. "Yes, I am. How... how did you know?"

"I just do. I can feel it."

Karen didn't want to talk, afraid words would diminish the wonder of this enchanted evening. Instead, she surrendered to the tide of contentment that engulfed them both.

He squeezed her, and his strong hand cut into her waist, arching her even closer, as if he feared letting her go. "This is insane." His lips touched the crown of her hair, his breath stirring her short curls. But he didn't loosen his hold, nor did he give an indication of wanting to let her go.

Evan interrupted them with the news that Matthew was ready to leave. "He's waiting for you at the front entrance," Evan told Karen.

Reluctantly, Karen withdrew from Rand's arms.

"Dad and I rode together," she explained unnecessarily.

"Stay," Rand murmured. "I'll take you home."

"Fine, fine." Evan gave Karen a boyish wink. "I'm pleased you two are enjoying yourselves."

Slowly, Karen led the way off the dance floor, giving Rand time to reorient himself.

"I'll only be a minute." She left Rand beside the chairs they'd shared before dancing and hurried to meet Matthew. Without bothering to explain, she gave her father a peck on the cheek and told him she had a ride home and would talk to him in the morning. Leaving Matthew looking slightly perplexed, Karen rushed to the main part of the reception hall and Rand.

But Rand was nowhere to be seen. For an instant, panic filled her until comprehension came. This time she was wise enough to seek her coat before venturing into the cold.

Opening the glass door of the balcony, she saw him standing at the railing as before. He didn't turn toward her, although she was sure he'd heard the door open.

"Rand," she whispered, suddenly nervous.

He turned to her then, his face a mask of indecision and inner turmoil. Karen yearned to run to his arms and kiss away his misgivings, to assure him that this unfathomable feeling between them was right and good. But she was frozen, overcome by her own apprehensions.

"Rand, please," she pleaded, "don't shut me out."

At the sound of her trembling voice, Rand's hard features softened, and he opened his arms to her.

Hesitatingly, she came, sliding her hands around his middle. "I know it's crazy. I don't understand it, either," she admitted, her voice low and faltering.

"I've never experienced anything like this." His voice was a strange mixture of anger and wonder.

Karen wanted to assure him this phenomenon was as much a mystery to her. "Me either, never."

"Oh, what the hell," he groaned out before his mouth crushed down upon hers in a kiss that was both fierce and hungry. His arms, folded tightly around her, relaxed as the kiss continued. Their reaction shocked them both. It was as if a charge of lightning had arced between them, jolting them. They broke apart abruptly, and Karen's breath came in uneven gasps. Had she been less unnerved, she might have noticed Rand's breathing was just as uneven.

Gently, Rand pulled her back into his arms, as if he needed to further test this sensation. This time, his kiss was tender and sweet, his mouth settling firmly over hers, drawing from Karen her very soul. When he finished, she was trembling and weak.

"Dear heaven," he moaned into her hair, "what's happening?"

Karen laid her head against his shoulder. "It's an enchanted evening, and you're the gallant Perseus," she whispered a little breathlessly, still caught in the wonder of his kiss.

"I'm hardly the gallant one," Rand said with a hint of sarcasm. "It's more like a bewitched Perseus held captive by the charms of the Lady Andromeda." His finger and thumb stroked her chin sensuously.

Mentally, Karen recalled the mythological tale. "Perseus rescued Andromeda, remember? She was doomed without him." Breaking from his hold, Karen examined the sky. "Rand, Andromeda's there." Excitement crept into her voice as she needlessly pointed to the heavens.

Rand's arms surrounded her again. "Of course Andromeda's there. Perseus needs her," he murmured, as if admitting to his own lacking. "It's been said she's very beautiful. May I examine her?"

Karen didn't understand his meaning until his fingertips began gently caressing the contours of her face, causing her to blush. Her eyelashes fluttered downward in confusion.

"Not only soft and delicate but very, very lovely." His husky voice was filled with reverence. Tucking a hand beneath her chin, he lifted her face while his mouth made an unhurried descent to claim her lips. Again, Karen's mind whirled to a new height of sensual awareness.

"I can see a distinct advantage to your blindness," Karen mumbled once the rapid beat of her heart stilled. "I'm no raving beauty."

Her hands, pressing against his back, could feel his corded muscles tense. It was wrong to mention his handicap. "I shouldn't have said that," she began haltingly, uncertain. Her teeth bit into her bottom lip as if she wanted to bite back the thoughtless words. "I have much to learn, Rand. I guess I'm afraid of making another stupid blunder."

"That was a compliment," he said stiffly. "You spoke to me as you would any other companion. You didn't attempt to rescue me or fall into the traps others do. People tend to think that because I'm blind I must also be mentally retarded. Nothing on God's earth irritates me more. Treat me as you would any other man."

"Why are you so angry?" Karen asked, attempting to hide the hurt in her voice.

Rand forcefully released his breath before a smile lifted the corners of his mouth. "I guess I do tend to stand on a soapbox every now and then. What I'm trying to say is that I don't want to be treated like a blind man."

"That won't be difficult for me. I have a hard time remembering. You move with confidence and show none of the outward signs. I thought the blind used white canes or Seeing Eye dogs."

"I have partial vision," he explained, and his mouth returned to an inflexible line. "A bad case of the measles as a child ruined my vision, and it's grown steadily worse over the years."

"Then you can see some things?" she questioned.

"Very little. Soon it will be as you mentioned—the white cane or the dog."

With infinite tenderness, Karen's hands cupped his jaw to bring his face downward so she could very gently kiss each closed eye.

Rand groaned and pulled her tightly against

him, his breathing ragged. "Oh, Karen," he murmured, holding her fiercely.

"Andromeda," she corrected with a smile.

They danced in each other's arms until there was no more music. They spoke little, embraced by the marvel of the night, creating their own world on a starlit balcony.

Rand was met outside the hall by a lanky, older man who stared curiously when he saw Karen was with Rand.

"Carl." Rand's grip tightened around Karen's waist. "I'd like you to meet the Lady Andromeda."

Without the slightest hesitation, the man grinned, showing crooked teeth but a ready, warm smile. "Pleased, I'm sure," he greeted her formally.

"I'm pleased, too, Carl. But to set the record straight, the name is Karen."

Carl grinned again and opened the back door of the car for them. "Where to?" he asked cheerfully as he started the engine.

"Karen," Rand whispered, "your address."

"Oh, of course." She supplied the information and leaned against the back of the seat until Rand's arm cupped her shoulder, drawing her close to his side. They rode in silence, bathed in a rare kind of contentment.

Sooner than Karen wanted, Carl arrived at

her apartment complex. Rand walked her to her door.

Gently, her hand stroked his face. "Thank you for the lovely, enchanted evening, Perseus."

Rand's kiss was tender and fierce all at the same time. Karen clung to him and moaned as the dizzy weakness spread through her limbs. A smile tugged at the corners of her lips, and she closed her eyes, surrendering to the charge of emotion Rand wrought in her.

Again, his mouth parted hers with a kiss as searing as it was devastating. "Goodbye, my lady," he murmured, and pressed his lips against her fragrant hair.

Karen opened the apartment door and floated inside, her heart singing a glorious melody.

Two

Karen woke to the smell and sounds of perking coffee. Reluctantly, she rose, looping the tie of her velour bathrobe around her slender waist. Stifling a yawn, she sauntered from her bedroom; the aroma of the coffee guided her into the small kitchen. She took a mug from the cupboard and poured herself a cup, ignoring the fact that the coffeepot was still perking.

"Ye shouldn't be doing that." A foggy voice broke through her consciousness. "You'll get grounds in your cup."

Surprise snapped Karen's eyes open. "Dad! What are you doing here?"

An injured look narrowed the faded hazel eyes. "'Tis a fine greeting for your father."

Karen lowered herself into the large overstuffed chair opposite Matthew. "Dad, as much as I love you, I must insist you stop entering my apartment like this." She schooled her expression against the pleading puppy-dog look her father gave her.

"Forgive an old man's curiosity." He lowered his gaze, suddenly looking lost and aged beyond his years.

"All right, Dad, you're forgiven. Gosh, you look awful."

His mouth deepened into slanted grooves of amusement. "Too many dances with a demanding widow." The look he cast her sent Karen into helpless giggles.

"Serves you right, old man."

"You're the bane of my life, you wicked child," he teased lovingly. "Now, tell me about the fellow you met last night. Do you like him?"

Self-consciously, Karen centered her attention on the steaming mug cradled between her hands. "Very much."

When she didn't volunteer any further information, Matthew probed again. "Well, go on. What's his name? When will you be seeing him again?"

"Dad, honestly." Karen stood abruptly, her fluid movements displaying a subtle grace. "Did you suddenly join the FBI? I don't like being interrogated. When will you realize I'm not your little girl anymore?" She didn't mean to sound so angry.

"Lass," Matthew pleaded, "you'll always be my little girl."

Karen's mouth thinned defensively until she realized her father's silver head had possessed only a salting of gray three years ago. He was aging right before her eyes. So much had changed in both their lives since her mother's death. Matthew had lost more than his wife and best friend. In the months that followed Madeline's unexpected death, Matthew's appreciation for life, his aspirations, even his personality had altered dramatically. Seeing her father now would have shocked someone who had known him three years before.

Shrugging in a gesture of defeat, Karen lowered herself into the chair and said, "His name is Randall Prescott; he's a professor at the university. I like him, Dad, better than anyone I've met." She paused, watching Matthew's reaction. "Rand is blind."

Matthew's eyes clouded with uncertainty. "Blind." His tongue tasted the word as if he found it unpleasant. "Lass, are you sure of your feelings?"

"I'm not sure of anything," Karen murmured dryly. "All I know is that I found him to be the most intriguing man I've ever met. Something happened last night, to Rand and me." She was quick to include herself.

"Something unusual. I can't even put it into words. It was almost as if our spirits communicated." She gave a short, embarrassed laugh. "I know that sounds crazy. Rand is tender and sensitive, but I don't think he exposes that side of his nature often. I...I think I was privileged to see that in him. And, Dad, he listens."

Matthew nodded. "I understand the blind often have an extremely good sense of hearing."

"Not hearing," she corrected. "He listens. He's not so caught in his own ego that he felt the need to impress me. He was interested in me as a person, my thoughts, opinions. That's listening, and there's a world of difference."

Matthew was studying Karen when she raised her eyes to his. "Yes, lass, that there is."

"Maybe it was the music or the champagne; I don't know." Her mind whirled with the memory of the electricity that had sparked between them.

"I think the lad was responding to the sensitive chord in you, Karen. Do you remember as a child you were always the one to rescue lost or injured animals? And several people, too, as I recall."

"Oh, Dad, I'm not rescuing Rand. For one thing, he doesn't need it. He's independent and proud. You've got to promise me you won't tell him about those things. He'd think I'm making a charity case of him. He'd hate that."

Matthew's eyes showed understanding. "I won't say a word," he assured her. "A man needs his pride."

Karen relaxed against the back cushion of the chair and sighed gratefully. "Thanks, Dad."

"As for Rand being blind, I would wish a sighted man for you, but that's my own selfishness. You're twenty-three now, and if you aren't an able judge of character, your mother and I have failed. I trust that in you, Karen. Your mother and I taught you well."

An overflowing love for her parents warmed Karen. "That you did, Dad. That you did."

Karen watched the phone all day, almost willing it to ring. She needed Rand to call just to confirm that last night had been as real to him as it was to her, and that the night hadn't been a romantic dream she'd conjured up with the moonlight. When he didn't, she couldn't contain her disappointment.

The next morning, Karen met her friend Audrey in a small coffee shop for their midmorning break. Both girls were employed by Tacoma's largest cable television service. Karen was the supervisor for the data processing department. Audrey had also been a candidate for the position but was relieved when Karen had it. Of the two, Karen had been the natural choice, having displayed tact, discretion, and forethought in a multitude of situations. Hiring a female supervisor had been only a token gesture by the company toward equal rights. Karen had stepped into a cesspool of resentment from her male counterparts. But it wasn't long before she grudgingly won their respect. She was good at her job and knew it.

"Do you realize I only have fourteen more days to finish my Christmas shopping?" Audrey announced as she set her cup opposite Karen's on the small table.

"Luckily, I did mine weeks ago," Karen said without meaning to sound like the methodical, organized soul she was. "I guess it helps when things have to be mailed."

"You'd have had it finished, anyway." Audrey sighed jealously. "I don't suppose I could interest you in fighting the crowds with me tonight? I thought we might have dinner out."

"Not tonight. Sorry, Audrey. I'm expecting a phone call."

"Someone I know?" Audrey quizzed with unleashed curiosity.

"No," Karen said pointedly.

Rand dominated her thoughts. Was he experiencing doubts about their evening? Had he decided this thing between them was the result of too much wine and music? Karen could only venture a guess at his musings. She had never longed to hear from someone so badly. Randall Prescott had her feeling very much like a schoolgirl praying that special boy would ask her to the prom. The melodious song in her heart was now replaced by an aching void of unanswered questions.

The phone was ringing when she let herself into the apartment that night. Karen dropped her purse and rushed to answer it, her heartbeat accelerating wildly. It was a carpet-cleaning salesman with a pitch for steam-cleaning her rugs. She definitely wasn't interested.

Audrey was at Karen's desk first thing the next morning. "Did you get your important phone call?" she asked before adding another pile of papers to Karen's workload.

"No, I'm afraid not." She tried to sound nonchalant and didn't bother to look up from her paperwork.

"I don't think you have much to worry about," Audrey said kindly. "He'll phone; only a blind man would be immune to your charms." Shock held Karen rigid. "I'll bet he phones tonight."

But Audrey was wrong. Rand didn't contact Karen that night or the next.

Friday night, Matthew was in Karen's apartment, waiting for her.

"Dad!" she admonished irritably. "The next time this happens, I'm going to have my lock changed."

"As soon as ye know why I'm here, you'll be singing my praises."

Feigning indifference, Karen hung her coat in the closet and went into the kitchen to make coffee.

"Don't you want to know what I found out about Randall Prescott?"

"Not particularly," she lied with an ease she didn't feel. Walking into her bedroom, she examined the contents of her closet.

"Karen, lass." Matthew followed her, his voice full of exasperation. "Hold still a minute. I want to talk to you."

"Sorry, Dad, I haven't got time now. I've got a date."

Matthew's puzzled features relaxed. "Ah, you're meeting Rand again."

"Not Rand." She pulled a crisp taffeta blouse and black velvet skirt from the closet, laying the outfit across her bed. "Jim Malloy is picking me up in an hour."

"Jim Malloy? What happened to Randall Prescott?"

Her throat muscles were so tight Karen could

barely speak. "I…I decided not to see him again. You were right about my feelings for him. Randall Prescott is just another lost kitten I wanted to rescue." She hesitated, then added, "Maybe it was a latent Florence Nightingale complex."

For several minutes, Matthew said nothing. "All right, Karen, you have to decide what you think is best."

"I have," she mumbled, returning to the kitchen to take the coffeepot from the burner. "Help yourself to coffee if you like. I've got to shower."

Scratching his head, Matthew watched Karen head for the bathroom. "Women," he mumbled. "They'll be a mystery to me on my dying day."

Karen had dated Jim Malloy before. He was what she considered a safe date. He was friendly without being pushy, considerate without being condescending. Jim's only problem was that Karen found him unforgivably boring. A hundred times during the dinner and movie, Karen wished she could change her feelings. What was she waiting for? Jim may not be a knight in shining armor, but he was nice. She was being stupid, she told herself as he politely escorted her to her apartment. Meekly, she submitted to his kiss. But it was hardly a kiss at all, more a brushing of lips.

Frustrated with herself, Karen opened her mouth slightly to deepen the contact, then moaned in disappointment. Why couldn't she feel what she had in Rand's arms? Why was she left with this void, this aching feeling at the touch of another man?

Jim reacted urgently to her initiative, crushing her against him. His hands fumbled with the opening of her coat, seeking her breasts.

Karen jerked away. "Stop it," she demanded. Her shoulders heaved with emotion, finding his touch repulsive.

"Come on. What am I supposed to think with a come-on like that?" His eyes were glazed with passion. "Let's go inside, talk this out." He pulled her back into his arms, his lips nuzzling her neck.

Again, Karen fought him. "No," she said sternly. "Not tonight. Not ever."

His dark, beady eyes filled with contempt. "You're nothing but a tease. Do you get your jollies by turning men on and then—"

"I think you'd better leave," Karen interrupted him, her voice steady and cold. Placing her apartment key between her middle and index fingers so its steel edge could inflict harm if necessary, she stared directly into his anger-filled eyes.

Jim didn't ignore the warning. "All right," he

spat viciously, "have it your way." He left in a hot temper, and Karen heard the squeal of his tires as he pulled from the parking lot.

After letting herself into the apartment, Karen leaned heavily against the closed door. What was the matter with her? A feeling of desperation encompassed her. She had led Jim to believe she wanted more than a good-night kiss and couldn't blame him for his reaction. For a fleeting second, she almost hated Rand.

"Damn you," she whispered harshly, and sat in the still apartment, staring into the darkness. She didn't move for a long while.

The next week passed with intolerable slowness, although Karen made an effort to keep busy. But each time the phone rang, her heart would beat expectantly. Each time, she tasted bitter disappointment.

Five days before Christmas, Karen received a long-distance call from her sister in Texas.

"Judy?" she asked with surprise. "Is everything okay?" With a limited budget, Judy rarely phoned unless it was important.

"I've got news too good for a mere letter," she began.

"You're pregnant?" Karen guessed immediately. "Well, for heaven's sake, have a girl this time, would you? Dad is driving me crazy for a granddaughter."

"Would you kindly shut up?" Judy chided with a laugh. "I'm not pregnant! I'm calling because Mike's being transferred to McChord."

"McChord Air Force Base?" Karen asked in disbelief. "In Tacoma?"

"Yes, silly."

"Oh, Judy, I'm so glad. You don't know how Dad and I've missed you."

"How is Dad?"

"Wait and see. I swear he's getting crazier by the day. Everything's changed since Mom died, especially Dad."

"I know." Judy sobered. "Even his letters are getting weird. There's a bit of bad news, too. Mike's being stationed in Thailand for a year."

"Judy, no." Karen's voice filled with sympathy. Her sister and husband had been separated before. It was a miserable time for them both.

"I guess I should be used to it by now. But at least this time I'll be by family."

"I'm so glad you're coming home." Karen tried to disguise the unhappiness in her voice.

"You don't sound right. What's wrong?" Judy and Karen were too close to hide anything from each other. Judy quickly detected the tiniest voice inflection and knew immediately things were not well with her sister.

Karen hesitated. How could she possibly explain? "I can't talk now. I'll tell you everything later. I promise," she said in a long, uneven breath.

"Count on it, sis," Judy said softly.

Judy's news was just the tonic needed to brighten Karen's Christmas. The news did a world of good for Matthew, too, Karen noted as they traveled to the Forsyths' on Christmas afternoon. Matthew seemed happier than Karen could remember since her mother's death.

At first Karen was a bit uneasy at her uncle's, fearing he would mention Randall Prescott, but the day passed comfortably, with no allusion to him or the party.

Everything moved very quickly after Christmas. Within a week, Judy and her family had arrived and moved into government housing. Mike, an aircraft mechanic, was due to fly out Monday afternoon, and he worked around the clock to settle his family before departing.

Karen volunteered to keep the boys Saturday night so the couple could spend the evening alone.

"Are you sure about this?" Judy questioned hesitantly. "James and Carter can be a handful."

"Of course I'm sure. I've been looking forward to this all week. If I were you, I'd make the most of my generous offer." She batted her eye-lashes seductively and watched her sister blush.

"I know, but—"

"No buts. Dad and I've got everything planned. We're going to have a great time, aren't we, boys?" Immediately, the two lively youngsters flew into the room, bounding with energy.

"Will you buy me a squirt gun, Aunt Karen?" six-year-old Carter asked.

"Carter," Judy warned in disapproval.

"We'll see." Karen affectionately ruffled the top of his blond head. "Get your sleeping bags loaded into my car. I'll be there in a minute." She placed her empty coffee mug in the kitchen sink and gathered her coat and purse. "Dad and I've got everything arranged. I'm taking the boys to a movie this afternoon, and then we're picking up Dad at the chess club. He's playing in that tournament this weekend," she explained needlessly. "From there we're going to have Chinese food."

Judy walked down the steps with her. "The boys will love it." Her expression softened. "Mike and I appreciate this more than you know."

Karen gave her sister an affectionate hug. "The pleasure's mine."

Judy laughed slyly. "Tell me that tomorrow afternoon; then I'll believe you."

"Come on, Aunt Karen. We're ready," the boys called from her compact Dodge, having rolled down the window.

"See what I mean?" Judy said.

The movie was a western comedy the boys ate their way through. After three bags of popcorn, two soft drinks, and a candy bar each, Karen wondered where they'd put the meal she'd planned for later.

"When's dinner?" James asked on the way to the parking lot.

"Dinner?" Karen gasped, then laughed, shaking her head at her nephew. "I can see I'm going to need groceries before we pick up your grandpa."

They made a quick trip to the neighborhood market, buying breakfast items and a few between-meals snacks, just in case the boys got hungry during the night, they told her.

Twenty minutes later, they arrived at the chess club. James and Carter looked around, curiously watching the players sitting at the long tables. Although the club was filled to capacity with nearly a hundred occupants, the noise level was surprisingly low. Glancing about the room, Karen easily caught sight of her father. He sat at one of the tables, intently involved in his game. She pointed him out to the boys and explained why they must be quiet and wait patiently. They sat in the back of the room, watching as each of the players made his move, then hit the clock, setting the other player's timer. The boys asked a couple of questions, but otherwise were content to sit and watch.

Briefly surveying the room again, Karen's attention moved to a table with three players. Instinctively, she stiffened, her emotions muddled and confused. "Rand." She spoke his name softly, her voice barely above a whisper. James and Carter glanced at her questioningly, but she didn't notice.

Rand lifted his head briefly, as though he'd heard, paused, then returned his attention to the game. But it wasn't possible for him to have heard her at this distance. His back, facing her, was held rigid and determined.

Drawing a deep breath, Karen's first reaction was anger and resentment. Yet there was a flooding relief, an elation just in seeing him again, even from a distance.

Karen continued to watch him for several moves with wry amusement. If he couldn't see the chessboard, how could he participate? It was soon evident Rand didn't use the board; the figures were moved for him on command by the third party. The entire game was played in his mind.

She experienced a twinge of pride when he

won the match. Her gaze followed him as he left the table and sauntered toward her.

"I'll be right back," she instructed her nephews. "Stay here."

She met Rand at the other side of the room. "Hello," she said evenly.

He showed no surprise, his face a proud mask. "Karen." He nodded in recognition.

"I didn't know if you'd remember me." She was being untruthful. He may not have contacted her, but he darn well hadn't forgotten her. She would have staked her life's savings on the fact.

"I remember you."

"I realize this is slightly out of the ordinary," she began haltingly, "but I'd like to know what I did wrong."

His brows drew together in a frown of confusion. "Wrong?" He repeated the word. "You did nothing wrong."

Of their own volition, her eyes were drawn to his face. It was unfair that he should have this much effect on her after all this time. For a moment, Karen thought he wanted to reach out and touch her, but he clenched his fist and held it stiffly at his side.

"Is it Cora?" At least she thought that was the name her godfather had mentioned.

Surprise flickered briefly over his expression.

"Uncle Evan mentioned her the night of the party," Karen explained shakily. "He said you usually attend social functions with her, and I thought there…there may be some romantic involvement."

His mouth thinned with impatience. "No, this has nothing to do with Cora."

"If I didn't do anything to offend you and… and if there's not another woman involved, I'd like to know what I did wrong."

He paused long enough to take his coat from the rack and slip it on. Pulling the gloves from the pocket, he clenched them tightly in one hand.

"My godfather also said you were a professor."

"What did you think I did? Sold pencils on street corners?" The tightening muscles of his jaw were the only evidence of anger.

"No, of course not." Oh dear, she was making a horrible mess of this. She inhaled deeply, hoping to calm herself and clear her thinking. "Listen, I'm going about this in the worst possible way. Could we start again?"

Ignoring her plea, he stepped outside, allowing the door to close before she could follow.

As childish as it seemed, Karen was tempted to stomp her foot and scream. Instead, she swallowed her anger and opened the door, stepping into the dark afternoon.

He had gone only a couple of feet. Karen allowed the door to shut before approaching him. "Rand," she said softly, "it doesn't matter to me that you're blind."

His posture remained rigid and uncompromising until Karen could tolerate it no longer. Without questioning the wisdom of her action, she placed a hand on his arm.

"Randall Prescott, would you kindly listen to me? If you had perfect twenty-twenty vision or if you were as blind as a bat, I'd still find you the most captivating man I've ever met."

His mouth twisted into a cynical smile that told her he didn't believe a word she'd said.

"It doesn't make any difference," she stressed again, quickly losing patience.

"Of course it makes a difference," he shouted angrily, startling Karen. He caught her shoulder in a tight grip. "Blast you, Karen. Blast you for being here. Blast you for—what the hell?"

Icy water hit Karen in the face. She gasped before being hit again. "James…Carter…stop it right now."

The two boys magically appeared and lowered their weapons. "I told you we'd get in trouble," Carter said righteously.

James ignored him. "I'm sorry, Aunt Karen.

I didn't mean to squirt you. I was aiming at him." He pointed a finger at Rand. "You moved in my way."

Rand handed his handkerchief to Karen. "You didn't mention you were related to the Dalton Brothers." A mere hint of a smile lifted the corners of his mouth.

Karen accepted the cloth and wiped the water from her face. "These are my nephews, James and Carter Turner."

"He was holding your shoulder real mean," James explained, hoping to vindicate his actions. "He looked like he was mad at you." Rand's imposing figure was enough to give the stoutest of men second thoughts. As far as Karen was concerned, the boys deserved a medal for bravery.

"You both owe Dr. Prescott an apology." Her voice was stern, but she worked hard to suppress a smile. Rand's face and shirt were soaked, and, feeling guilty, she returned his handkerchief.

"You're the one who got Aunt Karen in the face," Carter shouted angrily at his brother. "Now I bet we don't get dinner in the restaurant."

"It's all right, boys." A smile relaxed Rand's taut features. "You were right to protect your aunt."

"You're not mad?" James asked hesitatingly.

Rand allayed his fears. "No, but I want you to know I'd never do anything to hurt Karen."

Carter was obviously pleased with the turn of events and was quick to make peace. "I like her real well. She took us to the movie and let us eat all the popcorn we wanted and—"

"If you'd never hurt my aunt Karen, how come you were holding her shoulder like that?" James was not as easily appeased as his younger brother.

Rand didn't get the opportunity to answer, for Matthew burst upon the scene and demanded, "Where have ye been? I've been ready for five minutes. If it hadn't been for your purse, Karen, I wouldn't have known ye were even here."

"My purse!" Karen cried in dismay. She'd completely forgotten it in her eagerness to speak to Rand.

Her father handed the leather bag to Karen, who distractedly checked its contents for anything missing.

"I took the keys, so the boys and me will be leaving ye now."

"Dad?" she asked, her face a puzzled frown. What was he talking about? She was having dinner with him and the boys; it was what they'd planned. "I thought all of us were having dinner."

"Ye need to be discussing things with Rand,"

he said, dismissing her lightly. "Are ye hungry, boys?" he asked, grinning devilishly at Karen.

The boys gave a chorus of cheers, and with a hearty shout ran to Karen's car.

"Damn good game, Prescott. I demand a rematch."

Karen's attention swiveled to Rand, searching his face. "Did you have a match with my father this afternoon?" Karen could only imagine the things Matthew had been telling Rand. Indignantly, she turned her attention to Matthew to discover he had already left. Her small car purred as the engine came to life.

"Dad," she shouted angrily. "What about me?" Her full mouth compressed angrily as Matthew passed her in the street and gave her a friendly wave goodbye.

"I think he's abandoned you to my care." Rand's frown showed her he was none too pleased with her company.

"Well, don't look so thrilled," she snapped.

Silence followed until Rand began to chuckle, but the sound of his amusement did little to soothe Karen's ruffled feelings.

"This isn't funny," she insisted.

"Yes, it is." Rand broke into full rumbling laughter that shook his shoulders.

He continued laughing. "The fact is, I haven't found anything this funny in years." He contained himself somewhat. "Is it always like this with your family?"

"Sometimes it's worse," Karen stated dryly.

His amusement relaxed to soft chuckles. "Since Matthew's seen fit to throw us together, let's find someplace to talk."

Karen's spirits soared. This was what she'd originally wanted, to be with Rand. All at once, she wanted to kiss her interfering, meddling father.

They discovered a café several blocks from the chess club, and Rand ordered them coffee.

The silence stretched between them until Karen found her hands were trembling. Nervously, she clenched them together in her lap.

"Coffee hits the spot," she said with a false cheerfulness that sounded awkward even to her own ears.

Rand looked away. "Listen, Karen," he breathed forcefully, "I don't need to tell you I enjoyed meeting you and the Forsyths' party." He paused, his jaw tightening. "I thought you got my message when I didn't contact you afterward."

Karen gave a short, sarcastic laugh. "I got it, all right. I just don't happen to like it."

Rand placed his coffee cup on the table, and Karen noted how tightly he was clenching it. "Do you always get what you like?"

"No," she said lightly, "but not from lack of trying."

"I find this all flattering, but—"

"Flattering?" she interrupted.

"Very flattering," he said firmly. "But, Karen, you're young and pretty, and I won't have you wasting your time—"

"On a blind man?" she interrupted him again. "Squandering my youth and beauty—is that it?"

"Yes," he retorted angrily.

"Honestly, Rand, the next thing you'll be telling me is that I deserve a whole man or something equally stupid."

"That's exactly what I'm saying."

Karen nearly choked on her coffee. "I can't believe this," she said, keeping her voice level. "And even with this ridiculous attitude, don't you think I should be the one to decide? It's my life. I can squander it if I want." She ended with a short, nervous laugh.

"Not necessarily," Rand replied with a twinge of bitterness. "If you aren't going to use common sense, I must."

"What do you mean?" she demanded. "I've got terrific common sense."

Rand leaned against the back of the red booth. "You seem to be disregarding the fact that I don't want you, nor do I need you."

"I know that," she countered swiftly. She

glanced down at her coffee, relieved he couldn't
see the hurt in her eyes. "All I know is that I've
never experienced anything more beautiful than
that night with you. I don't even know how to
explain myself. But you can't deny it, Rand.
You felt it, too." She paused and waited for
him to comment, but he didn't. "It might have
been some crazy kind of magic that touched
us that night—the Christmas spirit of love and
goodwill. I can only guess." She hesitated. His
mouth had become the thin, hard line she recognized. Her back stiffened. Rand could say
what he liked; instinct told her he would lie.
She'd backed him into a defensive corner, and
he'd say anything to block her from his life. She
simply wasn't going to let him.

Suddenly, something changed in his posture. He relaxed somewhat; his mouth softened
enough for her to realize he was remembering. The enchantment of the party touched him
again, or perhaps he was as weary of the argument as she.

With his resolve weakening, Karen quickly
seized the opportunity. "I remember you once
told me you wished to be treated like a sighted
person. Well, I think you should know that
if you could see me, you'd notice I'm half
starved."

His mouth twisted into a fleeting smile. "Is that a hint?"

"No, it's a blatant attempt to con you into taking me to dinner." A full smile wrinkling the corners of his eyes told her she'd succeeded. "But before we do anything, I think we need to make an agreement."

A dark brow lifted itself expressively. "Such as?"

"We need a trial period to test our feelings. Everything was so crazy that night—the stars, the music, the moonlight."

"The champagne," Rand added dryly.

She nodded before realizing he couldn't see her acknowledgment.

"I guess I need to know if what I felt was real or some romantic dream." She hesitated before adding, "There would be no obligation on either side. Are you willing to do that?"

A veiled look came over him, one so transient and brief that Karen wondered if she'd imagined it. Then Karen knew. In that fleeting second, she knew. For all his resolve, for all his determination, he wanted her. He desired her more than she dreamed possible. At the same time, he hesitated; the flint hardness of his will and years of hard-wrought self-control warred with the tumult of his desires.

"No obligation on either side?" he questioned.

"None."

He ran a weary hand over his face, then slouched forward. "All right, Karen."

Three

"I've never known you to be particularly proper about this sort of thing," Judy said with straight pins between her teeth. "If I were you, I'd contact *him*. Turn," she directed.

Karen was standing atop her coffee table while Judy secured pins in the hem of the wild-rose-colored dress. "I think with any other man I would. But not Rand...I've done as much as I dare." It'd been two long weeks since their meeting at the chess club. Two of the longest weeks of Karen's life. A hundred times she was convinced she'd never hear from Rand again. Not even the gentle caress of his hand against her cheek when he'd dropped her off at her apartment or the promise he'd phone had been enough to dispel her insecurities. Karen had been so confident after that night. They'd eaten sandwiches at the café and drunk several more cups of coffee. They'd talked for what seemed only a short time but was actually hours. Karen told him of her childhood and friends, the pain of her mother's death—things she'd never shared with anyone else. Rand could not see her with his eyes, perhaps, but he could read her as if they'd known each other for years. Several times he paused and asked, "That's not all, is it?" or, "What were your feelings?" Karen had bared her soul to him as she hadn't with any other human. He listened intently when she spoke of her worries over Matthew and the changes in him since Madeline's death. He didn't offer advice, only listened with a knowing look that engendered confidence.

That evening, Karen learned bits and pieces of Rand's life, too. His mother lived in New York and worked for the state insurance commissioner's office. His father had died when he was eleven; Rand was an only child.

"Okay, let me stand back and see if this is even." Judy broke into Karen's thoughts. A warm smile formed. "This dress is going to be lovely. I'm proud of it." The vibrant jacquard material was being handcrafted for Karen as a birthday gift from her sister. "I'm sure if Rand could see you now, he'd be knocking the phone off the hook."

Karen didn't bother to correct Judy by saying Rand would never "see" her or the dress.

Judy's hand went to her chin as she continued to study Karen. "I don't think I've ever realized how much you resemble Mom. You've got her tilted nose and those warm, dark eyes. You're as beautiful as she was."

Karen had always been referred to as the "pretty" McAlister daughter. Judy was far from ugly, but her nose was a trifle too large, her mouth too full. But in the things that mattered, Judy Turner was the most beautiful woman Karen knew. "A lot of good a cute nose does me!" She smiled gently. "You've got the talent, while I'm stuck with two left hands. I could never sew anything this lovely."

"Sure you could." Judy dismissed her lack of confidence with a short shake of her head. "You'd better change. I imagine Dad's thoroughly tired of showing my boys chess moves."

Karen was in the bedroom when the phone rang. "I'll get it," Judy called. Karen stopped dressing, her pants zipper half-closed. Her heart beat expectantly, as it always did when the phone rang.

"No, this is her sister, Judy," Karen heard her sister say. "Yes, I am," Judy added. "I heard you three had quite an introduction. Let me apologize again for the boys." She laughed. "Just a minute. I'll get Karen."

Judy burst through the bedroom door. "It's him…It's him."

Karen released the breath she'd unconsciously been holding. A flooding sense of relief came over her until her knees trembled.

"Well, aren't you going to answer it?" Judy whispered fiercely.

"Yes…yes," she said again, hoping her voice sounded composed and confident, knowing it didn't. Slowly, to calm her nerves, Karen walked into the living room and picked up the phone. "Hello, Rand," she said softly.

"Karen"—his voice was curt—"how are you?"

"Fine, thank you." She was, now that he'd phoned. "And you?"

"Good." An awkward silence followed. "The Tacoma Actors Guild is putting on a play at the Pantages Thursday night. Would you like to go?"

"Yes, I would," she said with an eagerness that betrayed her.

"Wouldn't you like to know the name of the play?" he chided softly.

Karen silently berated herself. Why did she have to appear so anxious? "All right, if you feel it's important." Suddenly, she wanted to laugh. What did it matter if he knew how eager she was to see him? If she'd answered him in a completely monotone voice, he would have guessed her feelings, anyway. "What time should I be ready?"

Rand paused. "I'll be coming directly from the school and will probably be at your place around seven-fifteen. The play's at eight; that should give us plenty of time."

"I'll be ready." Karen felt like singing; she wanted to laugh and dance all at the same moment.

When he spoke, she could hear the smile in his voice. "I'll see you then. Bye for now."

"Bye." Karen replaced the receiver and glanced at her sister's curious face. Driven by a happiness she couldn't contain, Karen flung her arms around Judy. "How soon did you say my new dress would be ready?"

For the second time, Karen smoothed a wrinkle from her skirt. Nervous fingers toyed with the deeply veed neckline of the bodice, examining again the velvet ribbon, lace, and pearls of the ornate trim. The skill and patience it had taken to string each pearl between the delicate lace and ribbon brought a sense of awe to Karen. The dress was far more than a simple birthday gift; it was a labor of love.

Karen was ready early, absurdly so. Rand wasn't due for another twenty minutes, and already she had checked her appearance ten times in the hallway mirror. Careful attention had been paid to her makeup, although she seldom wore much, preferring the natural look. Styling her hair had taken the major part of an hour. If anyone had known she was going to such trouble for someone who could never see her, they would have thought she was crazy.

When Rand's knock came, Karen nearly jumped from her chair. Releasing a deep sigh of tension, she paused long enough to calm herself.

"Hello, Rand," she greeted cheerfully.

He moved into her apartment, and again Karen was struck by his basic masculine appeal. His face possessed character and strength.

"Karen," he said, his voice formal, "are you ready, or do you need a few extra minutes?"

"I'm ready." They were acting like awkward strangers meeting for the first time on a blind date. The analogy nearly sent her into nervous giggles. "Would...would you like something to drink before we go?"

Rand shifted; everything about him seemed controlled. "Thank you, no. The taxi's waiting."

Their conversation in the cab was so polite and stilted that Karen wanted to scream in frustration. This evening would never work with Rand's attitude. His formal greeting, the stiff conversation, indicated that although he was complying with his part of the agreement, he regretted it.

The seats for the play were among the best. The oppressive silence stretched between them while the theater began filling. Suddenly, Karen turned toward Rand and said the most ridiculous thing that came to mind.

"The rain in Spain stays mainly in the plain."

He relaxed. "The rain?" He arched a curious brow.

"That's right," she assured him coolly. "It stays mainly in the plain."

Against his will, Karen noted his eyes deepened into smiling grooves. "What makes you say that?" He was completely earnest.

"I could see what was coming. First you'd ask me if I was comfortable, and then we'd discuss the weather. It was either say something totally ridiculous or scream."

Amusement softened his expression. "I'm eternally grateful you didn't scream."

"You're most welcome. Now, are you going to enjoy the evening, or do I have to create a scene?"

For a moment, Karen thought Rand was going to laugh. "My mother warned me about women like you."

"I'm sure she did," she said resolutely after a pause. She shifted forward slightly. "Would you mind helping me with my coat? If I don't take it off now, I'll roast later."

His hand lingered as it cupped her shoulder in the briefest of contacts before following the sleeve and holding it stationary while she withdrew her arm.

"Thank you," she said softly.

His mouth moved into a lazy smile as he relaxed against the plush seat. "You're welcome." Tentatively, his hand sought hers, gently folding her slim one in his.

Karen settled into her seat, too. It was almost impossible to describe what a simple thing like holding hands with Rand did to her. Even a dictionary, Karen decided, couldn't define the pleasure she found in his company.

"Tell me about the play. It has the most curious title—*Deadly Vintage*." An aura of anticipation and excitement touched Karen, who enjoyed live performances above all else.

"A friend of mine wrote it," Rand began. "I think you'll find the plot intriguing. I won't spoil it for you by discussing details." He finished just as the curtain rose.

Rand was right; the plot was excellent, and the cast held the audience's full attention. The story revolved around a young man facing financial ruin, struggling against all odds to keep his business and family together. Karen felt herself tense as one complication after another fell upon the young man's shoulders. Right before the intermission, a second, older man was introduced, who promised to help the young man.

Karen sighed gratefully. "Things were beginning to look a little bleak there for a minute," she said to Rand.

He squeezed her hand and murmured cryptically, "Things aren't always what they appear."

"Oh, no?" She slouched against the back of her seat. "I thought you said you wouldn't ruin the story for me."

Amusement glittered from his dark eyes. "I wouldn't dream of it."

A sick feeling knotted Karen's stomach as the second part of the play unfolded. The older man agreed to pay all the younger man's debts on one condition. The young man must agree to have dinner with the older man. Sometime during the course of the meal, the young man would be offered wine. But the wine contained a deadly poison. No physical pressure would be applied to the man to drink the wine. If he chose to drink, it would be of his own free will. The man hesitantly agreed, but told the rich man he had much to live for and had no intention of drinking the wine. The older man amicably agreed that that was exactly as he wished it. Later, the young man learned this same agreement had been made many times over with others in the same financial difficulties. They, too, had agreed to the dinner with no intention of drinking the deadly vintage. In every instance, the men drank the wine and died.

The characterization of the rich man was portrayed superbly. The overwhelming force of his personality, his power of persuasion, had Karen sitting on the edge of her seat, wishing there was some way she could intervene and help the younger man. The play ended just as the wine was offered.

"That's it?" Karen gasped as the final curtain closed. "It can't possibly end there. What happened?" She turned anxiously to Rand. "What happened?" she demanded again.

"My dear Karen, I have no more idea than you."

The cast was called for three curtain calls, after which the theater began emptying. "Are you ready?" Rand questioned.

"No...not yet," Karen said stubbornly. Again and again, certain phrases and scenes played in her mind.

Rand shifted impatiently. "Karen," he said finally, "no one's coming to add a postscript. This is it."

"He didn't accept the wine," she said more

forcefully than she meant. She stood and reached for her coat.

"Is that so?" He was mocking her.

"Yes. If you examined the evidence, you'd realize it, too," she defended herself.

"It seems to me you're searching for a satisfactory conclusion. That sensitive female nature of yours insists upon a happy ending."

"Honestly, Rand, my sensitive female nature, as you call it, has nothing to do with this. What do you think he did?"

Karen had the curious sensation Rand was watching her, not with his eyes, of course, but with his other senses.

"I'm not sure," he said thoughtfully. "Why don't we go somewhere and discuss it? Have you had dinner?"

Karen hadn't; her nerves had been a jumbled mess most of the day, and although she hadn't eaten since lunch, she wasn't the least bit hungry.

"No, as a matter of fact, I haven't." Karen smiled to herself. She may not have much of an appetite, but she wasn't about to refuse an invitation from Rand.

Karen ordered a shrimp salad and coffee while Rand had apple pie. "Are you sure you wouldn't care for a glass of wine?" he teased after the waiter had taken the menu.

"Hardly!" She didn't bother to disguise her amusement. This was how she'd prayed their evening would be—a teasing banter between them without the steel-wall façade Rand had erected earlier. They discussed the play in detail; Karen argued her view while Rand, with clearheaded logic, proved exactly the opposite, that the younger man had drunk the wine.

"Now I don't know what to believe." Irrationally, she was almost angry with him. The matter had been settled in her own mind, and he had completely shattered her confidence. "I was perfectly content before."

Rand grinned that crooked little smile she'd seen only at rare times when he was especially pleased about something. Using some of the same rationale she'd used, Rand proceeded to prove that indeed the man had not drunk the wine.

Karen was astonished as she listened to him. Everything he said seemed perfectly sensible, sound, and reasonable, yet only a few minutes before he'd taken the opposing viewpoint.

"Remind me never to argue with you," she muttered.

"I've had more time to think about it, is all. And if past evidence is anything to go by, you hold your own in any argument. I certainly never intended to see you again, and look at us now."

Karen's eyes widened in hurt astonishment.

"I'd better phone Carl," Rand added after checking his watch. It was one made specially for the blind, and Karen was curious as to how it worked. "It's nearly midnight, and you're a working girl."

"Not tomorrow I'm not," she answered absently, trying to catch a glimpse of his wrist again.

"Is there some holiday I don't know about?" he asked, a teasing glint in his eye.

"Not a holiday, exactly." She placed her coffee cup on the china saucer. "It's my birthday, and the cable company gives their employees the day off with pay. Rather a nice gesture, I think."

"Your birthday?" His expression turned serious, as if he'd made a social blunder. "You should have said something."

Karen gave a tiny laugh. "I just did."

"You're twenty-four?" It wasn't really a question, and Karen didn't bother to answer. "There are twelve years between us. I'm far too old for you, Karen."

"My goodness, at thirty-six you must be sitting around just waiting to collect Social Security," she said with a mocking laugh.

She watched as he rubbed a weary hand across his forehead. "See what I mean? You effectively smash any argument I have against the two of us. Rather well, I might add."

While he phoned Carl, Karen excused herself to go to the ladies' room. She took longer than necessary, checking her appearance and applying fresh lip gloss and combing her hair. She felt so different with Rand and wondered if that tingling awareness between them affected her looks. Although she studied her reflection for several moments, she decided she looked exactly the same. Repressing a sigh of disappointment, she joined him.

"Carl is meeting me at your place in about twenty minutes," he told her in the foyer of the restaurant. "I have a cab waiting."

"That's fine," she agreed. "We'll have time for coffee."

Karen rested her head against his shoulder as they rode to her apartment. She could feel the roughness of his breath against her hair.

Once inside her apartment, Karen had no more desire for coffee than she had had for dinner. She hung up both their coats, suddenly feeling uneasy. "Make yourself at home. I'll get the coffee going."

As she turned toward the kitchen, Rand's arm

caught hers, drawing her back. "I don't want coffee," he murmured, pulling her close to him.

Without hesitation, Karen accepted his embrace, lifting her face to meet his kiss. It began sweet and gentle but deepened as he parted her mouth. The surge of passion that sprang between them was like a wind-driven wildfire. Her arms slid around his neck, her fingers wending through his hair.

His own hands were molding her hips and back against the contours of his body. It was a devastating kiss that left Karen as powerless as a newborn baby. It was very much like coming home after a long absence. They hadn't kissed since the night of the Christmas party, and Karen discovered that the magnetic attraction between them had only been enhanced by lapsed time.

Ripples of desire continued as Rand nibbled the sensitive cord of her neck. "Happy birthday, my lovely Andromeda," he whispered huskily.

"When I was a little girl," she began, her voice soft and trembling, "my mother insisted upon giving me kisses to count my birthday instead of spankings."

Karen could feel Rand's smile against her temple. "I'm afraid I haven't the restraint to kiss you twenty-four times without falling prey to other temptations."

Their lips met again in a fiery kiss that fused them together. Karen clung to him as the only solid form in a reeling world. When the kiss ended, she buried her face against his chest while he continued to rain soft kisses on her hair.

"Are you busy tomorrow?" he questioned, his voice no more even than her breathing.

"No," she lied skillfully. Evan Forsyth had invited her and her sister to lunch. Judy and the boys were preparing a birthday dinner for her that evening with Matthew. But nothing mattered, not friends, not family. Nothing save Rand.

"Can I see you, then?"

"Yes." She gloried in the eagerness of his request.

"Could you come to the campus—say, around eleven? I've got a class at nine-thirty."

Karen was too full of happiness to speak. He wanted to see her again soon. They wouldn't be separated for weeks, as had been the past pattern. "Yes, fine," she murmured, seeking the intimate taste of his mouth upon hers again.

A light tap, then the doorbell, interrupted them. "That'll be Carl," Rand murmured thickly, continuing to hold her shoulders.

Involuntarily, Karen swayed toward him, not wishing to break the contact. Gently, he kissed her lightly one last time. "Until tomorrow," he said, and paused. "My coat?"

"Oh, sorry." She fumbled awkwardly and withdrew it from the closet. Before she could add another word, he was gone.

The doorbell chimed impatiently several times the next morning at about nine-thirty. Karen rushed to answer it, her bathrobe knotted tightly about her waist.

"Dad," she exclaimed, letting him in. "What are you doing here? You're supposed to be working."

"'Tis a fine greeting for the man responsible for ye being here," he scolded her lovingly. "I've come to wish ye a happy birthday." He sauntered through the apartment to the kitchen and poured himself a cup of coffee.

"Did ye notice I rang the bell?" he said as he pulled a chair from the kitchen table and sat.

"I'm real proud of you, Dad, real proud." Her voice hinted sarcasm, but her smile negated any scorn by curving upward in a gentle smile. "Why aren't you at work?" she quizzed again.

Matthew deposited a second spoonful of sugar into his mug before answering. "I didn't feel like working," he told her indifferently. "A man needs an excuse to take a day off every now and then. And what better excuse than my lass's birthday?"

Karen poured herself a cup and sat opposite him at the tiny round table. She would have argued, but Matthew looked pale and drawn; perhaps a day's vacation was a good idea.

"Twenty-four years," he said with the glazed look that crossed his face when he was thinking of her mother. "Ye realize, when your mother was twenty-four, she was married, had Judy, and was pregnant with you."

Karen sighed heavily. She'd hoped to avoid another one of her father's tirades about her single status. "I know that, Dad."

"You're far behind her, lass. Even Judy had James and Carter before she was twenty-four."

Karen stood abruptly and emptied her coffee in the kitchen sink. "I know that, too," she said with a tight rein on her temper.

"There's not much time remaining before people will begin thinking of you as unmarriageable. I'd hate to see ye an old maid."

Karen's eyes ballooned angrily. "That's ridiculous," she spat impatiently. With storm clouds gathering, hands on her hips, Karen squarely faced her father. "Why is it you and I can't have a decent conversation anymore? You're constantly bugging me about getting married, and I'm not about to jump into a relationship to satisfy your whims. It's getting to the point I don't even like being around you anymore. Would you kindly lay off?" she said forcefully.

Her father's sad eyes met Karen's fiery gaze, and once again she noted that her father looked like a man well past his prime, a man without purpose. Taking deep breaths to control her temper, she offered him a weak smile. "I love you, Dad. Let's not argue, especially today. Okay?"

"Okay, lass." He responded to her smile with one of his own. "How was the date with Rand last night?"

Telltale emotions flickered across her face. "Wonderful. In fact, I'm meeting him this morning." Pointedly, she checked her wristwatch.

"I thought you were having lunch with Evan. He seems to have invited the whole family except me." If Matthew was hinting for an invitation, Karen wasn't going to issue one. Both girls were aware that although the lunch had been planned to correspond with Karen's birthday, the purpose was to discuss Matthew. The change in his personality over the past months had not gone unnoticed by his friends, and Evan was as worried as Karen and Judy.

"I am having lunch with Evan, but I'm meeting Rand first. That's why I've got to get moving."

"All right, lass, I'll see you tonight."

After surveying her wardrobe carefully, Karen chose designer jeans and a forest-green velour top. Since it was raining, she chose fashionable knee-high leather boots.

At precisely eleven, she entered Rand's office building.

"May I help you?" his assistant, an elderly gray-haired woman, inquired politely.

"I'm Karen McAlister. I have an appointment with Dr. Prescott."

The woman scanned the appointment schedule. "Yes, Dr. Prescott mentioned you this morning." There was a hint of censure in her tone, and Karen wondered what inconvenience their meeting was causing.

"Follow me, please." The cool smile displayed an efficient assistant's welcome. She paused outside the door. "Dr. Prescott's on the phone, but he's asked that you be shown in immediately. Would you like a cup of coffee while you're waiting?"

Politely, Karen declined. With her jittery nerves, she wasn't beyond dumping the contents across Rand's desk. She entered the office quietly so as not to disturb him. He gave no indication that he noticed her arrival, his full concentration directed at the person on the other end of the line. From the conversation, Karen assumed it was either his agent or his publisher.

She stood awkwardly in the middle of his office for several minutes, not wishing to sit, yet equally unwilling to feel like a child being disciplined. Her gaze swept the walls, resting on the degrees and certificates decorating the office. As she read their contents, her discomfort grew. On further investigation, she found Rand was the recipient of several prestigious awards. There was even a picture of him with the president of the United States. Nothing could have made her more aware of how separate their worlds were. A knot grew in the pit of her stomach as she read the contents of each framed accomplishment.

His achievements were astonishing, and Karen experienced a budding respect for the obstacles he'd overcome. She doubted there was any situation or crisis Rand couldn't surmount with patience and persistence. But her admiration did little to quell her uneasiness.

No wonder Rand questioned their relationship.

Depression, heavier than any yoke, weighted her shoulders. She actually felt her body droop under its burden. There could be no basis for a meaningful relationship between them.

Dismally, she moved to the picture window overlooking Commencement Bay. Oyster-gray clouds met murky waters in a thin overcast.

Only a few brave souls weathered the promise of rain, their sailboats slicing through the water. Yet Karen was blind to the picturesque beauty that lay before her.

"I'm sorry, Karen." Rand stood. "I didn't mean to be so long."

"No problem," she murmured abjectly, refusing to face him.

As soon as she spoke, Rand came to stand behind her. His hands rested lightly on her shoulders, drawing her against him. Gently, his lips touched her hair.

Karen suppressed an overwhelming urge to turn and bury herself in his arms. Instead, she stared at the world outside the window, feeling wretched and small.

"You're angry?" he asked, his tone suggesting surprise.

"I'm not," she murmured unhappily.

"Obviously something is troubling you."

Inhaling deeply, she faltered over the words. "I...I know why you asked me here today. It's shown me without words why you haven't wanted to see me again. I don't blame you. I understand now."

The grasp on her shoulders tightened, and, using his strength, he turned her to face him. "Just what are you implying?"

"I'm saying that I've never fully realized how

important you are. You're a respected professor, a noted author...a man of unquestionable financial insight. Do you realize I'm not so very different from the woman who ushered me into your office? Basically, I'm a nobody."

"A nobody?" He openly scoffed. "If that's the case, you've managed to wreak havoc on my life in short order." His expression didn't alter. "Do you really believe I invited you here to impress you with our differences?"

A lump rose in her throat, and she swallowed hard. It was ironic that she would argue with him without relenting a whit and then accept defeat after ten minutes in his office without a spoken word.

"Yes." Her voice trembled slightly.

"It was never my intention to see you after the Christmas party," he said deliberately.

"I'm aware of that."

"I said goodbye to you that night, and I meant it. But no woman has ever affected me the way you have, Karen. I'm not a romantic. The relationships I've had with women have been for the express purpose of satisfying a basic human need. That night with you shattered every preconceived idea I have regarding love and romance. You were gentle, sweet, and warm, more like the mythological Andromeda than a mere human. I knew then what could never be."

"I'm hardly a goddess," she interrupted with dry sarcasm.

He began again, his voice fervent. "I'm almost totally blind. I have no intention of maintaining a personal relationship with any woman. Not now, not ever. Even the attraction I feel for you will not convince me differently. You're special, Karen, and you deserve the best…certainly not a blind man."

Immediately, she bristled, but before she could say anything, Rand continued, "Maybe it's best we end this testing time now. That choice is yours, but I won't have you believing you're not good enough for me."

"Then why did you ask me here?" Her voice nearly failed her.

His features softened as the intensity left his face. "For this." He withdrew a jeweler's box from his pocket.

Hesitantly, Karen accepted the small case.

"It's not wrapped, but happy birthday, anyway."

Karen almost gasped when she lifted the lid. A lovely gold locket rested on a bed of purple velvet. It was old, but not an antique; the jeweler's box and style were outdated, but the locket was obviously new.

"It's beautiful," she whispered, lifting the

heart-shaped locket from the case to examine it more fully.

"Can you get it on okay? I doubt that I'll be much use."

"I think so." The chain clasped effortlessly as the locket fell naturally into place between her breasts. Karen longed to ask if the jewelry had been his mother's, but if it had any special significance, he wasn't telling her.

"Thank you, Rand. I'll treasure it always."

Softly, his hand caressed her cheek. As if it were suddenly too much restraint to keep her from his arms, he pulled her to him, hugging her fiercely. "Happy birthday," he whispered huskily.

His assistant's buzzer interrupted them, and Rand responded to the intrusion with a clear, crisp voice. The words were in a cloud as Karen gradually returned to the present.

"I've got to leave for a meeting," Rand told her reluctantly. "I'll phone you at the end of the week."

Karen smiled, her eyes dancing. "It seems I'm doomed to sit by my phone waiting for you to call."

Chuckling at her teasing sarcasm, he reached for his coat. "All right, how about dinner on Saturday? I'd like you to meet Cora Dibner. I believe Evan Forsyth's mentioned her."

Karen's spirits descended rapidly; she had no desire to meet the woman, but wondered what claim Cora had on Rand.

They walked from the building together, exchanging the teasing banter they both enjoyed. Halfway down the wide cement walkway, Rand stopped abruptly. "My book," he said with a shock. "I've left it in the office." He chuckled. "I've left my office a thousand times in the past seven years, and this is the first time I've forgotten my book. See what you do to me?"

Karen smiled, and her heartbeat raced with a new happiness.

"I'll have to go back. Karen McAlister, you'll be the downfall of me yet."

She watched as Rand progressed through the throng of students. "I hope I am," she said to no one in particular.

Four

Karen enjoyed her birthday lunch. The fettuccine complemented a lighthearted celebration, but it didn't take Evan long to come to the point of their meeting. He noted the changes in Matthew's personality, voiced his concern, and suggested the root of the problem was loneliness. Matthew needed to remarry, Evan concluded. Karen could feel the tiny hairs at the back of her neck bristle. No woman, however wonderful, could ever replace her mother. Selfishly, she did not wish to see her father marry someone else.

But the more they discussed the situation, the more both Judy and Karen were forced to acknowledge that perhaps Evan was right. It would take a readjustment in their thinking, but both were willing to make the effort as long as it helped Matthew—anything to change his present attitude.

Anxiously, Karen longed for the weekend and

the dinner date with Rand. Her curiosity regarding Cora Dibner was keen; only when she had met Rand's associate could she evaluate the extent of their relationship.

With each passing day, Karen discovered that Rand was coming to occupy more and more of her thoughts. Even the little things in life like shopping and cooking brought him to mind. While preparing a meal, she found herself questioning his likes and dislikes. When dressing, she wondered how he'd feel about a certain outfit she was planning to wear. Seldom did Karen consciously think of him as blind. Accepting his lack of sight was very much like accepting Judy's too-large nose. After a while, it became unnoticeable, a part of her person that was unconsciously overlooked.

When Rand phoned late and unexpectedly Wednesday night, Karen was reading and ready for bed.

"Karen?" A hint of doubt entered his husky voice.

"Were you expecting someone else to answer?" she teased.

He chuckled, his voice rich and low; the sound of his amusement contained an element of music. "No. I'm sorry to be phoning so late."

"That's fine. I was reading." He could phone

any time he wanted, Karen yearned to tell him, but to admit that would be revealing too much.

"I'm afraid I'm going to have to cancel our dinner date Saturday night." The regret in his voice communicated his own disappointment.

"Oh…" She sighed in frustration and absently fingered the gold locket he'd given her. Karen wore it continually, as if wearing it would result in some wonderful magic. She'd been so impatient to see Rand again, and the throbbing happiness she experienced just hearing his voice vanished with his announcement. It seemed their whole relationship was a series of setbacks.

"Karen, I'm phoning from Washington, D.C. I won't be back before Sunday."

"Washington, D.C." she gasped, and quickly glanced at the kitchen clock. "It must be two a.m."

"After two," he murmured tightly. "I've been tied up in one of those dreadful meetings that last forever and solve nothing." He sounded both tired and frustrated. "I suppose I should have phoned tomorrow night, but I needed to hear your voice."

Karen's spirits soared. The need to talk to her was something he admitted grudgingly, as if she were becoming a weakness he couldn't overcome.

"I'm glad you did call," she whispered softly.

"I like to hear your voice, too, but I'm sorry to miss meeting Cora." Karen flushed guiltily; her curiosity regarding his business associate had little to do with friendly overtures.

"You'll meet her," Rand assured her, then paused for a moment. "I've been invited to a wedding reception sometime next week. Would you like to attend with me? Cora will be there," he added, as if she needed an incentive.

"Yes, I'd enjoy that." Rand could issue an invitation to a funeral and she'd still experience a thrill of anticipation.

"I'll let you know what day and time later."

"That'll be fine. I don't have anything special planned for next week." She paused, then began hesitantly, "Would you like a kitten?"

"A what?" he asked in disbelief.

"A cat." She giggled. "My two crazy nephews brought home six kittens yesterday. Judy sent them to the store for a loaf of bread, and some lady was sitting outside the store with a box of kittens. The boys couldn't believe the cats were *free* and took all six. After all, they considered six free cats to be quite a bargain. By the time Judy returned to the store with the boys and the cats, the lady was long gone. In fact, Judy and I spent the evening posting 'free kitten' signs around the neighborhood."

"Those two rascals," Rand said, chuckling. "I suppose all six are females?"

"Do you have anything against females?" Karen asked with mock indignation.

"Not of late," he murmured with a chuckle. "All right, I'll take one regardless of sex."

"Judy thanks you, kind sir."

"Go ahead and choose one for me; I'll have Carl contact you to make the arrangements to pick it up. You can name it for me if you want."

"I'd like that." Already her mind was buzzing with several possibilities.

"I suppose I'd better let you get some sleep." His voice was warm and husky, creating in Karen anything but the desire to slumber.

"I suppose," she whispered on a sigh.

"Good night, my sweet Andromeda."

"Good night, Rand." She replaced the receiver and leaned back in the chair to savor every word of their conversation.

Karen met Carl Friday afternoon at Judy's. By the time he arrived, Karen still hadn't decided among the three remaining kittens. All were equally adorable, with feisty personalities and soft, cuddly fur. Carl stood by silently, refusing to be drawn into the decision making. In the end, James helped her choose the calico.

"The reason no one wants her is because she's

female," James declared, "but I think she's the best one."

"Well, that settles it," Karen said matter-of-factly. "Little calico, you're the one." She lifted the multicolored kitten from the box, examining her face carefully. "She's lovely. Thank you, James."

A hint of a smile touched Carl's wrinkled features. "Mr. Rand said you'd be choosing a female. Have you picked out the name?"

"Not yet," she said, frowning thoughtfully, "but I'm working on it."

"I like Super Pooper, because she's the one…"

"Carter, that's quite enough," Judy snapped, looking a bit abashed.

"Yes, Mom." The youngster's enthusiasm was immediately quelled, but his eyes sparked mischief.

Carl happened to catch Karen's eye, and she noted the difficulty with which he restrained his laughter.

The boys enthusiastically helped Carl load the kitten into the carrier he'd brought. Both made their farewells as if they were seeing their only sister depart to an unknown world.

"Such dramatics," Judy whispered with a sigh.

"Is Tuesday evening at seven convenient?"

Carl questioned as Judy and Karen walked him to the car, obviously referring to the wedding reception Rand had mentioned.

"That'll be fine. Thanks, Carl…for everything." She gave him a pleasant smile and waved as he pulled from the driveway.

On Tuesday evening, Karen was once again meticulous with every detail of her appearance. She chose a white taffeta puffed-sleeve blouse with a coordinating burgundy tiered skirt. The striking contrast of the two colors highlighted the dark, rich tones of her hair and winter complexion. Her face glowed radiantly with a light application of cosmetics, and her eyes were clear and sparkling. Although an emerald brooch was pinned to the neck of her blouse and she wore matching earrings, Rand's locket remained in place beneath the taffeta.

She looked and felt lovely, but again discovered her confidence slipping. Her stomach twisted with butterflies as she waited for Rand, not knowing how he would greet her. The gruff exterior he'd displayed at their first two meetings after the Christmas party was gradually wearing away. After her visit to his office and their telephone conversation, she knew he was mellowing. Intuitively, she recognized Rand was withholding part of himself, the part she'd witnessed the night of the party. Unexplainably, the barriers had been lowered that wonderful evening, and, with a heavy sigh, she wondered how long it would take to bring them to that point again.

Aside from the brief visit to his office, she recognized his game. Rand had purposely planned that all their times together involved others: the play, the wedding reception—even the dinner date he'd been forced to cancel had been arranged with Cora Dibner. It didn't matter; he could avoid being alone with her for only so long.

As before, Rand arrived promptly, and Karen was surprised to note that he came by taxi and Carl hadn't driven. Her heart raced with excitement. He was tall, strong, and handsome enough to be any maiden's dream.

"I'm early," he explained as Karen took his coat. "The reception isn't until eight."

"I don't mind. Would you like something while we're waiting?" She took the hanger from the closet.

"You wouldn't believe what I want," he murmured almost inaudibly, rubbing a weary hand across his face.

"Pardon?" She stopped, her hand suspended in midair.

"Nothing…it wasn't important." He stood awkwardly in her tiny entryway, suddenly looking unsure.

"The most comfortable chair is to your left," she said lightly, hoping he wouldn't find her directions a form of rescue.

He smiled gratefully. "Thanks." He located the large overstuffed chair and sat down.

"Would you like something to drink?" Nervously, she placed a strand of hair behind her ear. She didn't keep a large supply of beverages on hand and could only hope she had what he wanted.

"Coffee, if you have it."

"I do."

"Why the sigh of relief?"

"What?" Although halfway to her kitchen, Karen turned back toward him.

"You sighed like you were afraid I'd ask for a Smith and Currens."

"I did?" she asked blankly. "I didn't even realize it."

"Don't worry. Blind men rarely drink anything stronger than coffee," he remarked.

Waving her hands excitedly, Karen marched to his chair and sat on the ottoman. "There, you did it again." Her voice was high-spirited. "I was trying to explain to Dad about your ability to listen."

"I don't have any unusual listening ability," he contradicted her.

"Of course you do," she said dramatically. "Do you remember when I bumped into you on the balcony the night of the party?"

"I'm unlikely to forget it." He smiled rakishly.

"You knew right away I didn't have my coat because my voice trembled."

Rand straightened, his posture suddenly defensive and stiff. "In case you weren't aware of it, nature often compensates for the lack of one sense by enhancing another. I've been told my hearing is extraordinary."

"Honestly, Rand." She shifted irritably. "That's what Dad said. One would think you of all people would know the difference between hearing and listening."

A frown creased his brow. "I don't understand what you're saying."

Exasperated, Karen expelled her breath unevenly. "Okay. The other day in your office you apologized for being on the phone so long. I told you I didn't mind, but immediately you detected there was something wrong—"

"My dear Karen, it was obvious you were upset; your voice was low and tight—"

"But that's it," she interrupted. "I've used that same tone of voice a hundred times, and no one has ever guessed my feelings. You did because you *listen*. I mean really *listen*. That's so rare, Rand. It's probably the most appealing thing about you."

"You mean my dashing good looks don't faze you?" he teased.

"Well, not entirely." Her long, thick lashes fluttered downward in a disconcerted movement. "The other day, I invited Dad to dinner. He gets home earlier than me, so I asked him to come to my apartment, take the casserole from the fridge at five o'clock, and put it in a three-fifty-degree oven. Dad put it in at five hundred degrees at three-thirty. Needless to say, we went out for hamburgers. If I'd given you the same instructions, I have no doubt they would've been followed explicitly."

Again, he dismissed her theory. "People misunderstand one another all the time. My ability to hear or listen or whatever," he said a little impatiently, "is a figment of your imagination."

Karen studied him, the tiny crow's-feet that appeared at the corners of his eyes, the salting of gray hairs at his temple. The deep-colored eyes stared back at her, but how much he could see, Karen could only guess.

"All right, Randall Prescott"—she gave in graciously—"you're right. The whole thing is a wild, unreasonable assumption." She should have known better. With his defensive attitude, it was unlikely he'd admit to anything that set him apart or made him different.

"Did you say something about coffee?" he reminded her gently.

"Oh, sorry." She apologized quickly and stood, returning to the kitchen.

Both cups were full and steaming when she returned and sat opposite Rand.

"By the way, have you come up with a name for the cat?"

"Yes," she told him uncertainly, "but I'm not sure you'll like it."

He arched a curious brow. "Well?"

"Everyone knows a cat is supposed to have nine lives, but did you also know there are said to be nine heavens, nine regions of hell, nine heads of the hydra, nine muses, nine crosses, nine orders of angels, nine worthies…and…"

"A cat-o'-nine-tails," Rand injected smoothly.

"Right"—she laughed nervously—"and seeing how there are so many nines in the world and all, I thought I'd name her Number Nine." She shifted in an anxious movement. "What do you think?"

"My birthday is October ninth."

"See, all the more reason," she said, laughing lightly.

"I don't suppose this decision has anything

to do with the fact that we met December the ninth?"

"Absolutely nothing," she lied smoothly, then giggled because it was so obvious she was lying. She should have known better than to try to outwit Rand. He was too perceptive, too astute.

He gave her a full smile that did crazy things to her heartbeat. "I knew you'd come up with some connection to our first meeting."

Suddenly, they were both quiet, each entangled in the memories of that night. Perhaps it was a time Rand would as soon forget. Perhaps it was even an embarrassment to him now. But for Karen it was more an assignment with destiny. She smiled secretly to herself; Rand would laugh if he could hear her thoughts. Yet more and more she had come to think of their meeting as preordained and as irrevocable as uttered vows.

Rand spoke first. "I think Number Nine, although a bit unusual, will be a fine name."

They talked for a while longer, laughing over the antics of James and Carter with the comfortable ease of friends. More than once Karen found herself thinking that Rand would make a wonderful father. Picturing Rand with children did funny things to her stomach. The mental image of him holding a child, their child, was more intoxicating than any wine. Karen quickly reined in her imagination. Taking their relationship any further than the moment was a dangerous pitfall she was going to avoid.

The taxi delivered them to the Elks Lodge, where the reception was being held. With Rand's arm placed gently around her waist, they entered the crowded room. At Rand's request, Karen signed the guest book for them both.

Seeing so many people put Karen on edge; meeting a roomful of strangers wasn't her idea of a romantic evening.

"Why so tense?" Rand whispered after the first couple of introductions.

"I'm sorry," she said, surprised at how tight her voice sounded. "I'm a little ill at ease when I don't know anyone. Does it show that much?"

"Only to me." A suggestion of a smile touched his eyes, as if he were suddenly aware he'd almost admitted his listening ability was more astute than others. "I'm not particularly fond of these affairs myself."

"Rand!" A tall, attractive blonde propelled her way through several people to greet him with an affectionate hug. "You made it, after all."

Hastily, Karen removed her hand from Rand's arm as the woman stepped forward.

"Aren't you going to introduce us?" she questioned, eyeing Karen resentfully. She was older than Karen, perhaps thirty, and carried herself proudly, confidently. Her metallic-blue eyes were piercing.

"Cora"—Rand's voice was warm and friendly—"I'd like you to meet Karen McAlister. Karen, this is Cora Dibner."

"Pleased, I'm sure," Cora said, but her look belied any pleasure.

Karen's heart beat painfully; she had hoped to be friends with Rand's associate. He spoke of Cora so often—often enough for her to suspect their relationship went beyond business interests. Now that they'd met, there was no denying the jealousy in Cora's eyes. Or that she was in love with Rand.

"I'm pleased, too." Karen smiled in return and nodded, as worthy opponents often do when facing each other.

A glimmer of respect entered Cora's eyes. "Are you one of Rand's students?" Her voice remained friendly, but the whiplike flicker of her gaze cut into Karen.

Involuntarily, Karen stiffened. This woman was after blood in their first round. Cora must have known Rand was uneasy with their age difference. She laughed lightly, giving the impression such a question was ridiculous.

"Hardly. Are you?"

"You wouldn't believe the things he's taught me."

The mocking words hit Karen with the impact of a hammer pounding a nail. Were Rand and Cora lovers? A sickening knot twisted her stomach until she thought she might be sick.

Rand cleared his throat in embarrassment. "Yes…well, I think it's probably time Karen and I went through the reception line. If you'll excuse us, Cora."

"Of course." Cora's smile, directed at Karen, was full of malice. "Nice meeting you, *Carol.*" She purposely used the wrong name as a means of telling Karen she wasn't worried. Her grip on Rand was secure; she had nothing to fear from Karen.

"You, too, *Nora,*" Karen said in kind, her eyes narrowing. "I hope we meet again."

Rand frowned. "Cora seems to be out of sorts tonight." He dismissed his associate's behavior. Karen wanted to cry because making excuses for Cora's behavior showed he cared.

"We all have off days." She swallowed tightly. "Would you mind if we had something to drink before going through the reception line?"

"I think we could both use something," Rand said.

Two glasses of champagne clouded the encounter with Cora. Another glass and Karen saw the whole incident as comical. Rand was distracted by friends and didn't notice how many times her glass was refilled. But Karen, held protectively to his side, was always introduced and included in the conversation. Another half glass and her former nervousness dissipated; her smile was friendly, her laughter quick, and her eyes sparkled.

"We better do the honors while we can," Rand suggested after a while. "Are there many people left in the reception line?"

"Hardly any," she told him, and had the crazy desire to giggle. Rand honestly believed people really listened. She'd show him.

Rand introduced her to the first person in the reception line, one of the ushers, a brother-in-law of the groom's. Bravely, Karen looked him directly in the eye and smiled sweetly. "I'm very pleased to meet you," she said, shaking his hand. Although her eyes never left his face, she added impishly, "The elephants are loose."

Rand's arm stiffened its hold around her waist, biting into her tender flesh.

"How do you do?" the usher responded politely to her warm smile. "I'm so glad you could come."

"I am, too." Her eyes sparked with mischief. "I am, too," she repeated.

Before proceeding farther, Rand's low voice growled in warning, "Karen, what are you doing?"

She laughed saucily. "I thought you said people listen," she whispered back. "I'm just proving a point."

Undaunted by Rand's tight grip around her waist, she made the same obscure announcement to the next member of the wedding party. Again, nothing was said or noticed. Apparently, wild elephants on the loose were not of interest to the entire wedding party. The only one to add anything to Karen's ridiculous statement was the last woman in the line, who proudly boasted she was the one who introduced the wedding couple.

They'd gone no more than three paces from the line, just out of earshot, when Rand demanded in a low snarl, "Just how many glasses of champagne have you had?"

Karen had to stop abruptly in order to think, causing Rand to bump into her. She would have stumbled forward if not for his grip. "Three." She hiccupped loudly. "Oops, sorry. No, I think it was four." *Could it have been five?* she mused; she'd lost count.

"I'm getting you out of here." The words were muted, and for a moment Karen wondered if she'd heard him correctly.

"Gee, I was just beginning to have some fun." She hiccupped again.

"Karen, don't say another word," he warned.

Her lips moved to protest, but somehow the words couldn't get past her tongue.

"Promise me you won't say a word to anyone."

She hiccupped again. "How can I promise you that when I'm not supposed to talk?" She shot a quick glance at Rand. Why was he so interested in leaving all of a sudden?

The cold air outside the lodge stunned Karen, although she felt flushed and warm. The street was deserted, the sidewalk bathed in shimmering moonlight. It reminded Karen of the night she and Rand had met. The stars were shining, but to gaze at them did funny things to her equilibrium.

Suddenly, Karen had the overpowering desire to dance.

"Rand," she whispered seductively, waltzing a few steps ahead of him, "may I have the pleasure of this dance?" She curtsied politely.

"Karen."

Was it impatience she heard in his voice? It must be the hiccupping; it was driving her crazy, too. "Then for heaven's sake, kiss me," she demanded. "That'll stop them."

"Stop what?"

Rand was definitely on a different wave-length, Karen mused, and giggled on another hiccup.

"The taxi's here," he told her, his hand gripping her upper arm firmly.

"But, Rand, I want to dance," she pleaded. Her lashes fluttered downward suggestively.

Rand ignored her and directed his attention to the driver. "I need to get some strong coffee into her."

The driver laughed as Karen hiccupped again. "Drive-through or restaurant?" he queried.

"Drive-through…definitely a drive-through." Again, the driver laughed.

"But, Rand, I don't want any coffee." She forced herself to concentrate on him. His eyes were anxious, disturbed. That worried Karen. Was he angry? One arm cupped her shoulder protectively, as if she needed his strength to sit upright. The fingers on his other hand drummed a nervous tempo against the seat.

Her eyes narrowed. "You think I'm drunk," she said in an accusing, high-pitched voice that suggested absurdity.

"My dear Karen, another glass of champagne and I'd have had to carry you from the reception."

Karen giggled. "Honestly, Rand, I'm as sober as a"—she couldn't think of anyone sober—"a judge." She waved her finger wildly, as if to prove her point.

Rand snorted, but his mouth deepened into grooves as he suppressed a smile.

Karen's fingers crept to his face, caressing his jaw, outlining his mouth with the tips of her fingers. "Please kiss me," she whispered softly as her hands moved up and over his shoulders, meeting behind his neck, urging his mouth to hers.

At first, his kiss was slow and gentle, but Karen moaned, seeking deeper contact. She wasn't disappointed when his lips hardened and parted hers. Desire seared through her blood until Karen thought she would drown in the pleasure of it.

As he released her, she felt the cold air come between them and rested her head against his shoulder.

"Either your kisses are more potent than I remember," she said, smiling lazily, "or else I shouldn't be closing my eyes, because the whole world goes into a tailspin."

She could feel Rand's smile against her hair. "Then by all means protect Mother Earth and keep your eyes open."

Karen groaned when her alarm rang early the next morning. The shrill ring triggered a burst of pain in her head. When she sluggishly sat upright to turn off the offending noise, she thought her head would burst.

Slouching against the pillow, she groaned again, holding her head. Looking around her, she found her normally neat bedroom in a shambles; clothes littered the floor, and one shoe sat on the windowsill, while the other remained hidden from view. She could vaguely recall singing and dancing around the apartment as she undressed. Taking deep breaths, she calculated the consequences of staying in bed, but the call of responsibility soon moved her into action.

Once fortified with a cup of strong coffee and two aspirin, Karen showered and dressed. She lifted her eyebrows expressively when she located her second shoe in the bathroom sink.

Fifteen minutes before she was due to leave for work, Rand phoned.

"How are you feeling?" His tone was laced with concern.

"Don't ask." She tested her voice for the first time and found her tongue thick and her words husky. "I think I'll live if my head quits pounding." Memories of the night remained hazy; she could recall Rand saying something about coffee and a beautiful, sensuous kiss in the back of the taxi, but beyond that, the evening was veiled in her mind.

"I'm almost afraid to ask, but did I do anything out of the ordinary last night?"

She could hear his soft chuckle. "My dear, I've got enough information to blackmail you for life."

Her breath was forced from her lungs; things were worse than she imagined. "I was afraid of that."

"Just remind me never to argue with you again. I didn't know what lengths you were willing to go to to prove a point. From now on, if you insist most people don't really listen, I won't question the fact."

Karen laughed, wondering where she got the courage to pull anything so crazy. "I think everyone in the whole wedding party probably heard me but was too shocked to respond."

Rand did little to relieve her anxiety. "I think you've made your mark among my friends."

Karen's face remained tight and strained when the smile died. "I believe," she began awkwardly, "that I owe you an apology. I'm so sorry, Rand. I don't know what got into me."

"I'd say it was several glasses of excellent champagne," he interrupted smoothly.

Karen closed her eyes for a moment. "I feel terrible about the whole thing."

"Honey"—Rand's chuckle was warm and sincere—"I can't remember when I've enjoyed a wedding reception more."

Five

Thursday afternoon, the sky was thick with threatening gray clouds that promised rain. Karen rushed out one door, down half a block to the restaurant, and in another, where Judy was waiting.

Her sister waved as soon as Karen entered. "Hi." Judy smiled in greeting as Karen sat opposite her in the small booth. "I've got our order in; it should be here any minute."

Karen sighed appreciatively. "Thanks, Jude. It works out great when you can get here early and order for me. It's been a madhouse this morning. I didn't even think I'd get here at all for a while."

"It's a darn good thing you did." Judy laughed, her eyes sparkling. "You should have seen the look the waitress gave me when I ordered *two* chef salads."

Karen laughed, a natural release from the tension of a hectic morning. "What have you heard from Mike?" she asked just as the waitress brought their salads.

"Not much. He's miserable, counting the days till he can come home, but he loves his job and the challenge. Sometimes I wish he was like a normal husband with a nine-to-five job, but he isn't. It's something I learned to accept long ago."

Judy and Mike had been right for each other from the time they started dating in high school. Karen was almost envious that her sister had been so fortunate to have found her husband as a teenager. It was a fact Matthew had often used to convince Karen she was being overly choosy. But since Karen had been seeing Rand regularly, Matthew had all but ceased his demands.

"You're seeing quite a bit of Rand, aren't you?" Judy questioned unexpectedly. Her voice held a worried note, and she watched Karen closely.

"Not as much as I'd like." Karen was surprised by her sister's attitude. "Does it bother you that Rand is blind?"

Judy shook her head, quickly denying the implications. "Of course not."

"Then why the censure?"

"Karen"—Judy hesitated, looking uncertain and more than a little uncomfortable—"I know you like Rand, but I don't want to see you hurt.

I think you should tread carefully with this relationship."

Karen studied her sister thoughtfully. *Liking Rand.* That was the understatement of the year. Judy and Karen had always been close, even as children. Almost five years separated them—a big difference when Judy was a sensitive teenager and Karen was a pesky younger sister. Even then, they had shared a special relationship. Yet, in all her years, Karen couldn't remember her sister acting in quite this manner.

"Things between Rand and me are going even better than I'd hoped," Karen told her sister, but Judy avoided eye contact, paying inordinate attention to her salad. "Rand's just beginning to be comfortable with me; the defensiveness over his blindness is almost gone. More important, I sense he is accepting me into his life. It's more than I'd hoped to accomplish in such a short time. Although"—she smiled before continuing, as if she'd overcome an important hurdle in their relationship—"tonight is the first time we'll be alone together. His reader is sick, so I'm going to the school after work and read his students' papers to him. He's promised me dinner. More than a fair trade, I think."

Judy didn't mince words. "Do you love him?"

Karen didn't even hesitate. "More than I thought it was possible to love any man."

"Does he know it?" Judy still hadn't touched her salad.

Karen sighed heavily. "I'm sure he does." A hundred times, Karen had longed to speak freely of her feelings, but this was a sensitive area, and she knew she must be patient. Not that she doubted his feelings.

"If you love him, why don't you tell him?" An odd expression crossed Judy's face.

"I can't, Jude. Rand doesn't want to hear it. I know that's difficult for you to understand, but for now that's the way things have got to be."

Judy shifted uneasily, again giving the impression something was weighing heavily on her mind. "Are you sure of his feelings?"

Karen's soft mouth curved into a smile. "All right, sis, what is it?"

Judy looked all the more uncomfortable. "What's what?"

"Obviously, you've seen or heard something about Rand, and you're worrying yourself sick over it."

Judy sent her a sidelong glance, and her shoulders drooped forward in defeat. "Am I really so easy to read?"

Karen smiled with sudden humor. "My heavens, I've seen James and Carter less obvious."

Judy laughed, too, her smile more relaxed. "I was on campus the other day and saw Rand," she began, her fingers nervously twisting her napkin. "I knew who he was the minute I saw him. I mean, you've talked about him enough."

Karen knew Judy was taking a couple of classes at the university, and it didn't surprise her that she'd seen Rand.

"Only Rand wasn't alone." Her eyes met Karen's briefly. "There was a woman, a tall blonde, with him, and Karen, I may be an old married lady, but I know a come-on when I see one. This woman was definitely on the make, and Rand was eating it up."

"That's Cora Dibner," Karen interjected on a long breath. "You don't need to tell me she's after Rand. The lady and I have met."

Judy sighed, visibly relieved. "I've been so worried. I don't think I've ever seen any woman that smooth. What gets me is that Rand seemed oblivious to what was happening."

Karen smiled ruefully. "As far as Cora is concerned, I think Rand is more aware than he lets on. I don't doubt that he can see through that layer of cool sophistication. Rand's no fool."

Judy studied her sister pensively. "For your sake, I hope you're right."

Karen went directly to Rand's office after work. She stopped only once at the ladies' room to check her appearance. Her lipstick had faded, and she freshened the honeysuckle-rose color and ran a quick comb through her hair. Impishly, she sprayed her favorite fragrance to the pulse points of her neck. Rand had commented once on the delicate white ginger scent she wore. He was sure to detect it again and smile at her womanly wiles.

"Karen?" Rand's welcome was both a question and statement.

She let herself into his office; the door between his office and his assistant's was open, anticipating her arrival.

"Yes, it's me." Her heart beat a little quicker each time she saw Rand; he was everything she'd ever wanted in a man, more than she dared dream she'd find. "I hope you're not one of those slave drivers who won't allow coffee breaks? I'm dying for a cup."

"Now, just a minute," Rand teased. "There's nothing in our contract about coffee breaks." His expression altered. "Hmm, you smell good."

Excitement churned inside her. "Good enough to kiss?"

"Definitely." His voice was both low and hoarse.

Karen floated into his open arms with the sense that this was where she belonged. The whole world could be at war, but as long as she was loved by Rand, there was nothing that could touch her. She wound her arms around his neck, marveling at the strength of his muscular shoulders. His mouth took possession of hers. It was a demanding kiss that parted her lips. Rand kissed her cheek, her ear, her eyelids, and when she groaned, he returned to her mouth. Again, Karen was trapped in a whirlpool—the warmth, the taste, the feel of him—until it didn't matter if she ever surfaced.

With her head resting against his chest, she could hear the erradic tempo of his heart and knew he was as affected by their kiss as she. His breathing was hoarse and uneven; his arm gently caressed her back as if he couldn't bear to let her go.

"I have the feeling that either we start work now or we'll spend the entire evening exactly like this." The reluctance in his voice thrilled Karen.

She agreed, knowing she'd have a difficult time speaking, almost regretting the need to pull herself away from the hazy fog of pleasure that blurred her mind.

Reluctantly, Rand withdrew his arms and sat on the corner of his desk, giving Karen his chair, the most comfortable in the office.

When Karen began reading, her voice was shaky and a bit awkward, but gradually she gained confidence, and her tone became steady and sure.

Rand's transformation from lover to professor was accomplished with an ease Karen envied. Could it be he wasn't as affected by their lovemaking as she? Quickly, she dismissed the thought. Rand had lived with rigid self-control all his life. He was as affected as she; it just didn't show.

After reading each paper, Karen wrote Rand's comments on top of the page. She found his grading system to be stringent and uncompromising, but she was impressed by his fairness and judgment. His comments to the students included some form of encouragement, but he didn't offer praise unless it was warranted.

At the end of the first stack of papers, Karen's throat felt dry and scratchy.

"You need a cup of coffee," Rand commented before she began reading the next pile. "There's usually a pot of coffee in the kitchen."

Karen stood, stretching her tired muscles. "Do you want a cup while I'm at it?"

"I never drink and grade papers," he admonished her jokingly.

Karen laughed and suddenly couldn't resist kissing him. Rand's reaction was immediate, pulling her into his arms and deepening the contact. "Karen," he groaned in warning, "you're not making this any easier."

She straightened. "Sorry." Even now her

voice sounded faintly raw from the lingering effects of his kiss.

"Karen"—he stopped her—"bring me a cup, after all. I'm going to need something to clear my head." His eyes were warm and loving. "You don't exactly encourage the sensible side of my nature. You know that, don't you?"

"Yes, sire," she answered saucily.

The next hour and a half were interrupted only by coffee breaks or when Karen had a question about something Rand needed to explain. They found they worked well together. Everything about them was right, Karen mused on a happy note.

"Didn't you say something about buying me dinner?" she asked quietly after marking Rand's comments on the last paper.

Rand walked across the office, flexing his shoulder muscles as if he were stiff. "I had Dorothy pack us a dinner. I hope you don't mind." His back was turned toward her.

"Dorothy?" Was there someone besides Cora she needed to contend with?

"Dorothy is Carl's wife." Rand paused, taking a deep breath before raking his hand through his thick hair. "The thing is, Karen, I don't like to eat in restaurants. Most blind people don't. It presents an unfamiliar environment."

Karen could have bit her tongue. How could

she have been so thoughtless, so insensitive? She had made it necessary for Rand to admit something he considered a fault. It was a humbling experience that set him aside and made him appear different.

Karen was appalled at her own insensitivity. "You know, I thought I smelled something delicious when I came in this afternoon. But I couldn't very well accuse you of hiding prime rib in your desk drawer."

The tension faded from Rand's face. She'd done right by making light of his admission; apologizing would only have made the situation worse.

"Dorothy did pack roast beef. Between the ginger scent you're wearing and the aroma of beef, I've been like a man on the rack for the last two hours."

Karen drew a deep, troubled breath. "Well, which one of us would you like to devour first?"

Rand groaned and reached for her, pressing a hard kiss upon her lips. But before he allowed it to develop into something deeper, he straightened. "I think you'd better unpack the picnic basket before you find out. Carl put it in the coat closet against the wall."

Whoever Dorothy was, she certainly knew how to cook. The meal couldn't have been prepared or packed more efficiently. Karen spread the tablecloth on the thick carpet of Rand's office and unpacked their meal of French dip sandwiches made on crusty French bread. The beef, sliced thin, was piled on so high Karen doubted she would be able to fit the sandwich in her mouth. She poured steaming au jus into the bowls while Rand removed the cork from the bottle of wine.

"Fresh strawberries!" Karen exclaimed enthusiastically. "Where in heaven's name did she ever find strawberries this time of year?"

Rand chuckled, the sound of his laughter brightening the evening. "I never ask. The woman's a wonder."

As they ate, Karen's admiration for Dorothy grew. Everything was perfect, beautifully done.

"Ready for a strawberry?" Karen questioned, but when Rand reached for one, she restrained his hand and instead carried it to his mouth. Hesitantly, Rand accepted it, rubbing the juice from his chin as he bit into the tender pulp.

"Your turn," he insisted. Her lips trembled as his fingers touched her mouth, awakening within her a whole range of sensual sensations. When they kissed, the taste of fresh strawberries, mingled with the wine, was more potent than anything Karen had ever experienced.

His hands fell away from her shoulders as

Rand took a deep, uneven breath. "I think we'd both benefit from some cold air."

Karen's breath wasn't any less jagged. "Yes," she said, finding her voice barely audible against the tightening in her throat. She was so intoxicated with her love for Rand that tears stung her eyes.

The night was cold and dark; the wind bit into Karen as they walked hand in hand across the campus. They needed the cold to put things into perspective, to remove them from the passion of the moment.

By mutual agreement, they chose the paved pathway leading to Commencement Bay. Lovers of all ages had used the path leading to the beautiful waters of Puget Sound. There was a freshness in the air, and Karen inhaled deeply, finding the faint odor of salt water pleasant. The wind whipped her hair across her face, but she ignored the cold, taking delight in the simple pleasure of walking along the beach with the man she loved. There was no need for words; it was their spirits that communicated. Rand needn't voice his love; his arm, pressing her possessively against his side, warding off the brunt of the wind, said it far more effectively than words.

Karen was too full of pleasure to speak. When Rand paused, stopping to gaze into the dark, cold night, the only sound was the pounding of the surf against the smooth beach. Somehow Karen found herself in his arms; their lips met in a fiery kiss that fused them together. Karen clung to him. He was her love, her life for all eternity. Nothing could ever make her happier than what she was at this moment.

"Oh, Karen," he groaned, his voice deep and pained.

"No." Her fingers hushed his lips. "Don't talk." She buried her face against his coat, feeling the roughness of his breath against her hair.

He walked Karen to the parking lot where she had left her car. Again, he kissed her, a feather-light kiss that teased and promised.

"I'll be out of town this weekend," he whispered into her hair. His finger gently circled the small of her back in a sensuous movement that melted her bones. "Meet me at the airport Sunday afternoon."

Karen seemed incapable of speech; his physical impact on her was complete.

"I'd like to show you my home." Gently, he released her from his embrace.

"I'd like that," she managed, extracting herself from his arms.

He opened the car door for her. "Drive carefully," he cautioned, and Karen watched him from the rearview mirror as he stood in the lot until she was safely on her way.

Sunday afternoon, Karen chose a dark chestnut-colored wool skirt and a cream cashmere sweater with a single gold strand woven in a delicate pattern to wear to the airport. She debated between boots or her heels, finally deciding on the knee-high leather boots because it was raining. She was adding the final touches to her makeup when Matthew spoke.

"Ye seeing Rand again?" His eyes showed appreciation for Karen's natural good looks.

She turned sharply at the unexpected intrusion, her eyes angry. "Dad, you did it again. When will you learn to knock?" It was more a statement of indignation than a question.

"Lass"—Matthew gestured helplessly, showing impatience with himself—"I keep forgetting."

It was impossible to be angry with her father when she was in such high spirits. "Well, try, won't you?"

Karen knew he was just as likely to walk in unannounced the next time.

"Ye seeing Rand again?"

Karen knew he wouldn't be satisfied until she'd told him about their dinner date. "Yes, I'm meeting him at the airport. We're having dinner at his home near Graham."

"You love him, don't ye, lass?" The question was more of an announcement, and Karen couldn't deny the obvious. Besides, Matthew was a master in the art of inquisition and would have dragged the words from her one way or another.

"Yes, I do…very much." Self-consciously, she lowered her eyes.

Matthew flashed her a proud smile. "Randall Prescott will make me a fine son-in-law. You've chosen well."

"Dad," Karen said with indignation, "you're rushing things. There's been no talk of marriage."

"Aye, but there will be," he said confidently.

Karen laughed impishly. "If I have anything to say about it, there will be." It was impossible to imagine life without Rand now.

"Ye know, the course of true love between your mother and me wasn't smooth. I had my problems getting her to agree to marriage."

Karen was shocked. As far as she knew, her mother and father had been madly in love from the time they'd met.

Her eyes must have shown her surprise. "Your mother was the most beautiful girl I've ever seen. I took one look at her sweet face and knew I wanted her for my wife. But I was thirteen years older than Madeline, and her parents didn't take kindly to a thirty-one-year-old man courting their teenage daughter."

"Little wonder." Karen knew, of course, that thirteen years separated her parents, but she'd never thought of it in terms of eighteen and thirty-one. Nor had she been aware that her grandparents had voiced any objection to her father.

"Not only did Madeline's parents not trust me, but yer mother had more beaux than a movie star. For a while I became discouraged, but in time I was able to win her over."

"But, Dad, what did you do?"

Matthew followed Karen into the kitchen and bent close to whisper: "I've never told another living soul this, but I tricked your mother into marrying me. But not for a day did she regret it."

"You didn't," Karen said with a gasp.

"Aye, but I did."

Karen could hardly believe what she was hearing. "How did you trick Mom?"

His whole face broke into a wide, mischievous grin. "I whisked her away. By the time we arrived in Idaho, she'd agreed to be me wife."

Karen felt the sudden need to sit down. "You mean to tell me you kidnapped Mom?"

Matthew laughed boyishly. "It was hardly

a kidnapping. I was just helping her make up her mind."

For a moment, Karen was dumbfounded. "Honestly, Dad, you astonish me."

"Aye, it was a brave thing, but your mother never regretted it. I knew she loved me."

Karen would have said more, but her doorbell rang. When she introduced Carl to her father, the two men shook hands respectfully. Karen slipped on her full-length leather coat, and the three left together. Matthew was invited to Evan and Milly Forsyth's for Sunday dinner and promised to give them Karen's love.

The drive to Sea-Tac Airport was accomplished in a companionable silence. Carl seemed to be a quiet, gentle man about the same age as Matthew. His loyalty to Rand was unquestionable. They parked with relative ease and waited in baggage claim.

Rand was the last passenger to arrive, and again the sight of this virile man sent her heartbeat racing. She experienced the urge to rush to him and hug him fiercely; instead, she walked forward almost hesitantly and whispered his name.

Smiling, Rand immediately held his arms open for her. Karen was there in a second, as if it were the most natural place in the world for her to be.

"Welcome home." Carl greeted him with a smile.

"Thanks, Carl. It's good to be home." He smiled at Karen, his look tender and warm. Slipping his arm around her waist, he added, "Very good indeed."

After a thirty-minute drive, Carl turned off the road and into a long driveway. Karen watched with growing anticipation for the first view of Rand's home. Having him invite her to his home held a special significance; Karen felt it was almost symbolic. The final defense was being lowered.

She tensed slightly as they drove down the winding driveway. The first view of the house left Karen awestruck. The house was magnificent, a long, sprawling, contemporary rambler. The large grounds were landscaped meticulously. Another smaller home stood in the distance and roused her interest.

Carl answered her unspoken curiosity. "The smaller house is for me and the missus." His voice was filled with pride.

Holding her hand, Rand led her into his home. He was confident and sure in the familiar surroundings; his movements were precise and made with ease. They stood in the elegantly tiled entryway that led to a sunken living room. The fireplace was lit, the flames reflecting a warm, welcoming glow. A solid-oak dining-room table was set in the formal dining room off the spacious kitchen. The candles flickering from the table's centerpiece cast dancing shadows across the bone china and crystal glassware.

"It's beautiful…everything's beautiful." Karen spoke with a sense of awe. Rand's personality was stamped in every piece of furniture, every room. He had allowed her into the inner sanctum of his life; this home was his pride. Shown a hundred different locales, Karen would have immediately known this house belonged to Rand.

Carl brought in the luggage with the instruction to call when Karen was ready to leave.

The door had no sooner closed behind him when Rand turned to her. Very gently, he took her face between his hands. "I've missed you." He bent forward and kissed her with a fierceness that spoke of longing and frustration. Karen responded with an urgency that matched his own. It had always been like this between them; that jolt of charged electricity that sparked the fire of awareness until every nerve sang with life.

He whispered her name, and then slowly released her. With her eyes still closed, Karen swayed toward him. Rand chuckled and kissed her again fleetingly before placing an arm around her shoulders and leading her to the dining room.

"Let's eat," he murmured, "while I'm still in control of my senses."

Karen would have willingly forgone the meal to have remained in his arms.

As before, Dorothy's cooking was superb. Karen couldn't remember ever tasting chicken tetrazzini with such exquisite flavor.

After the meal, they decided to have their coffee in front of the fireplace in the living room. Karen cleared the table and brought in the coffee on a tray already prepared by the efficient Dorothy.

Enjoying the warmth of the fire, they talked for a long time. With her head resting against Rand's shoulder, his arm around her, Karen discovered they shared several interests. They enjoyed the same authors, and both played chess and were addicted to mellow music.

While Karen returned the coffee tray to the kitchen, Rand placed a CD featuring Rimsky-Korsakov's *Scheherazade* into his CD player. The melodious sounds filled the air as Karen returned.

"May I have the pleasure of this dance, kind sir?" She curtsied before him, her wool skirt brushing the cream pile carpeting. "As I recall, the last time I did this I was rudely rejected."

"The last time you wanted to dance, we were on a downtown sidewalk with half of Tacoma looking on," he remarked, his voice full of humor.

Karen giggled, lifting her arm in entreaty, her body already swaying to the music. "You have no sense of adventure," she chided him softly.

He gathered her in his arms, his body moving rhythmically with hers. "Every time I'm with you, it's an adventure." His hand arched her spine closer, pressing her body intimately against the hard length of his.

Karen closed her eyes and nestled against Rand, glorying in the dizzy emotions he could arouse within her.

They danced, although they barely moved, content to be in each other's arms, lost in a world created only for them.

When the CD finished, they didn't move. The pressure of Rand's fingers at the base of her neck lifted her face upward to meet his descending mouth. Obediently, Karen's lips parted as she molded herself against him, responding with all her love to his deepening kiss. Her hands around his neck were winding a path through his hair, pulling him closer, igniting a slow-burning fire of passion between them until Karen ached.

The fierceness of his lovemaking awoke

yearnings Karen had never experienced, and she moaned in surrender as Rand lowered her onto the couch. His hungry mouth claimed hers again and again while his hand slid intimately over her body, seeking the satin contours of her breasts. Caught in the powerful undertow of her love, Karen felt herself drowning in an ocean of sensations.

Suddenly, Rand raised his head, holding himself away from her. "No...no," he uttered harshly, his voice hoarse and barely distinct.

Suddenly bereft, Karen tried unsuccessfully to bring his mouth back to hers, struggling against him, holding him as if her life depended on his.

Angrily, his hand closed over her wrists, firmly pushing her away. He stood and strode across the room, his fingers raking his hair.

Bewildered, Karen sat upright. She was shocked by her wanton behavior, but equally disturbed by Rand's rejection. Her cheeks flamed red from embarrassment and the lingering effects of desire.

"Rand?" It was a muffled cry from her heart.

Rand sat down slowly beside her, gripping her shoulders, forcing her against him.

"Karen, oh, Karen..." His jagged breath was rough against her ear. "It would be the most natural thing in the world to carry you to my bed and love the very life from you. But there would be the reality to face in the morning. Heavens knows I want you. And right now you think you want me, too, but someday you'll thank me for this."

"Oh, Rand..." Her voice wobbled, and she clung to him as if being in his arms would prevent the new day rising. Let there be no tomorrow if she couldn't have him.

Gradually, the desire ebbed, leaving her confused.

Six

"Thank you, I had a wonderful evening," Karen lied with an ease that amazed her.

The elderly hostess gave her a sympathetic smile. "Do come again."

Karen smiled weakly in return; the lump in her throat had grown so thick she could barely swallow. She slipped into her coat and stepped outside, where Carl was waiting. Rand remained inside for several minutes. Why had he stayed? He couldn't possibly be enjoying this. Did he wish to humiliate her further?

Carl glanced at her quizzically. The strain about her mouth and the hurt in her eyes were impossible to hide; she looked away, not wanting anyone else to witness her pain.

Rand joined them.

The ride to Karen's apartment was completed in a wearisome silence that crowded the large vehicle.

Pride held Karen stiff. What had happened? Why was Rand doing this? Things had been strained between them ever since the night he'd invited her to his home. They had been together several times since, and on each occasion he'd grown less civil, less courteous. He was erecting the granite wall between them again, and Karen didn't know if she could stand it.

This evening's party had brought to a climax everything that was wrong between them. Perhaps it wouldn't have been such a disaster if Cora hadn't been there, but Rand had made every effort to make Karen uncomfortable. His attitude from the very beginning had been chilling, but once they'd arrived at the party, it was almost as if he'd forgotten her. He sat with Cora, rarely leaving her side, making excuses to touch her, attentive in a way he had never been with Karen.

Karen chatted with several people, attempting to ignore his behavior, but there could be no pretending when Cora flashed her a look of triumph. A look as loud and clear as if she'd shouted it across the room: Rand was hers, had always been hers, and would forever be hers.

"I suppose you're waiting for an apology?" Rand asked stiffly.

They sat as far apart from each other as possible. "Not unless you feel like making one."

His laugh was short and humorless. "I don't."

"Then it would be pointless, don't you think?"

He shrugged as if an apology were of little consequence either way.

When Carl stopped in front of her apartment building, Rand straightened. "Would you escort the lady to her door, Carl?" The command was issued as if he couldn't bear to even say her name.

Carl muttered something unintelligible under his breath. Karen didn't wait for him to open her car door, jerking it open with a violence that demonstrated the pain of this final humiliation. Had she come to mean so little to Rand that even the courtesy of taking her to her door was beyond him?

Her lips trembled, and she avoided Carl's probing gaze. "Don't bother, Carl," she spoke in a tight, shaky voice. "I'll let myself in."

"It's no problem, miss."

As he inserted the key into her lock, Karen looked back to the car. The streetlight illuminated the dejected, solitary figure inside. Rand had slouched forward, his hands covering his eyes, portraying the picture of a man weighted by an intolerable sadness.

Carl's eyes followed Karen's. "He's been under heavy pressure lately. I'm sure he didn't mean anything."

Tears welled in Karen's eyes; she blinked with the effort to hold them back. Gently, she placed her hand on the older man's arm.

"Thank you," she said softly.

"Well, you certainly look in better spirits than you did the other day." Judy took a slice of carrot from the tray; James and Carter quickly followed suit.

"Hey, you guys, cut it out. There won't be anything left for Rand." She slapped their hands playfully, her eyes laughing. "I feel a whole lot better." Her eyes met Judy's briefly, knowingly. "I don't know what's up with Rand, but you can darn well bet I'm going to find out."

Judy laughed at the spark in Karen's eye. "You know, I almost pity him."

"How do I look? Do you think I'm overdoing things a bit?" She was wearing the birthday dress Judy had made for her. Not only was it one of the loveliest things she owned, but it boosted her confidence, reminding her of the support and love of her family.

"You're lovely," Judy assured her quickly.

"Aunt Karen, can I light the candles?" James questioned enthusiastically.

"Not yet; I don't want to light them until right before Rand gets here."

Both boys gave a disappointed sigh. "All right, I'll tell you what." She playfully tousled the tops of their heads. "The next time you're over, I'll have a candlelight dinner just for you."

"Can I light the candles?" James asked again.

"Naturally."

"But I'd rather have hot dogs than the smelly stuff." Carter wrinkled his nose at the odor of marinating steak.

"I'll have you know that smelly stuff cost me a week's allotment for meat," Karen informed them indignantly. "But don't worry, if you want hot dogs, then we'll have hot dogs."

The boys gave their approval with a loud cheer.

"I think we'd better go. I don't want to be here when Rand arrives," Judy said after checking her wristwatch.

Karen was grateful. "Remember to keep Dad occupied and out of my hair. It would be just like him to drop by for a visit, and I don't want any interruptions."

Judy winked dramatically. "Gotcha."

Suddenly, Karen was unsure of herself. Was she doing the right thing by forcing the issue? "Are you sure everything is right? The wine goes with the meal? The candles aren't too much? I'm not overdressed?" she asked all in one giant breath.

Judy shook her head dismissively. "Settle down. Everything is perfect; you have nothing to worry about."

"You're sure?" Karen glanced around nervously.

"I'm sure. All right, boys, let's visit grandpa." The boys ran ahead. Impulsively, Judy gave Karen a hug. "Good luck. Everything will work out beautifully; wait and see."

Karen wished she possessed the same confidence. Her fingers toyed with the gold locket Rand had given her as if she could draw solace and courage from its presence.

She was placing the finishing touches on the salad when the doorbell chimed. Karen hurriedly wiped her hands on the apron, then carelessly tossed it aside. Pausing for a moment, she closed her eyes to compose herself.

It had been only a few days since she'd last seen Rand, and yet her nerves raced at the physical impact of his presence.

"Hello." She greeted him with false cheerfulness and slid her hands up the lapels of his coat, anticipating his kiss. He hesitated before claiming her mouth. The kiss lacked tenderness or warmth, and Karen avoided another.

"I hope you like marinated steak," she said

casually as she hung up his coat. His face looked tight and a little pale. "How about a glass of wine?"

Rand smiled faintly. "Do you have anything stronger?"

"Do you think you're going to need it?" she challenged.

He ignored the question and sat in the overstuffed chair Karen had purchased for its deep-cushioned comfort. But Rand didn't relax; his posture remained tense and straight. "I'll take the wine."

While Karen poured for both of them, her gaze rested briefly on Rand. His facial features, which suggested strength and pride, seemed more pronounced. She watched as he wearily rubbed the back of his neck.

When he accepted the wine, his eyes held a dark, unreadable light. As she sat opposite him, he withdrew a neatly wrapped package from his pocket.

"This is for you," he said tightly.

Karen took the package, her eyes widening with surprise. Was the gift a means of apologizing for his rude behavior these past weeks? Karen relaxed against the back of her seat, suddenly wanting to sing.

Her fingers fumbled as she removed the ribbon and paper. It was a jeweler's case; the name of an exclusive and expensive store was stamped in gold across the top. She hesitated for only a moment before opening the lid.

On a bed of red velvet lay a shimmering gold bracelet, one more beautiful than anything she'd ever hoped to own. She longed to go to him, touch him, thank him as only a lover could. Instead, she whispered softly, "I've never seen anything this beautiful. Thank you."

When she glanced at him, she was surprised to note his wineglass was empty and she'd yet to taste hers. She was reaching for her glass when Rand spoke.

"The bracelet is my way of saying goodbye." The words, savage and tender all at once, were spoken softly.

Karen was so shocked she nearly dropped her glass; part of the wine emptied into her lap.

"What did you say?" She was so stunned she hardly noticed the sudden wetness.

"I said," he began coldly, deliberately, "this is goodbye."

Karen searched his face, praying she'd find some evidence that would tell her he was joking. "You don't mean that."

He gave one of those abrupt, mirthless laughs she had come to hate. "I mean it. We're both adults, and I believe we can do this in an adult manner. I won't be coming here again, and I don't want you to make an effort to see me."

"Why?" The lone word was wrenched from her.

"Damn it, Karen, I'm tired of playing your romantic games. I think it's time you grew up." His body was stiff with determination, his face expressionless, a tight mask.

"I can't understand why you're doing this." Her eyes pleaded with him, implored him.

"Why did you *make* me do it like this? The things I've done to you in the last two weeks couldn't have driven the message home more forcefully. Why do you have to be so damn stubborn? Why did you keep coming back for more hurt, more humiliation?" Although his voice was forceful and steady, it contained an element of pain, as if he found it as difficult to say the words as it was for her to hear them. "I don't want you. Can I make it any plainer than that?" He was shouting at her, then paused and began again, more controlled. "I don't like myself when I'm around you."

Karen's throat muscles were so tight she didn't know if she could breathe much longer. "Please, Rand, don't do this to us." Where was her pride? She choked on a sob but swallowed it before it could escape and humiliate her further.

"*You* did this to us," he accused her harshly.

"You and your trial relationship. Why in the hell couldn't you leave things alone? I didn't want you then, and I don't want you now. Do you understand?"

Hurt and anger flashed from the depth of her dark eyes. "I understand, all right. You're only half a man, a blind coward, and I've discovered I want a whole man. Would you just leave?" she screamed, but her heart was begging him to stay.

He stood abruptly. "I've heard enough."

"While you're at it, take the bracelet with you." She threw it at him, box and all; it hit his chest and bounced onto the floor, spilling onto the carpet.

"And this." She jerked the locket from her throat, snapping the delicate gold chain, and threw it at him with all her strength. Rand flinched as it hit him in the face.

"Now, will you get out of my life?"

She ran to her room; she'd be damned before she'd let him see her tears. She sat on her bed, her hands twisting nervously in her lap, noticing for the first time the stain of the spilled wine. The dress, the lovely dress Judy had spent so many hours sewing, would be ruined. In a panicked rush, she unzipped it, allowing it to fall to the floor. She needed to soak it, or the stain would never come out.

She turned blindly and crashed into the open closet door with a sickening thud. Pain stunned her for several seconds before she slumped to the floor, releasing a cry of anguish and pain. The tormented cry of a wounded animal.

"Karen, Karen…" Suddenly, Rand was there, rushing toward her. To her horror, he caught his foot on the edge of the carpet and stumbled into the room. Karen reached out to help him regain his balance, but her action sent him crashing to the floor. Rand grabbed her bare waist and twisted his body so he would absorb the full brunt of the fall. They lay on the floor, their arms and legs entwined, catching their breath.

Rand spoke first. "Are you all right?"

Her tears became sobbing hiccups. "No."

He shifted their position so he was above her. "Where's the pain?" The tender concern in his voice made her weep all the harder.

"My heart."

He groaned as his arms curved around her, gathering her against him while his lips unerringly located her eyes, kissing away each salty tear. He began at the corner of her face, kissing her forehead, her chin, her neck, her ears, before claiming her mouth in a kiss that was as fierce as it was devouring. Karen lifted her mouth to meet his, her trembling lips parting in anticipation.

They clung to each other, their hearts beating wildly as one. His lips followed a slow path down her neck and bare shoulder while his hand wandered over her back, over her hip, molding her soft, womanly body to the hardness of his. Their mouths met, slanting across each other with hungry impatience.

Karen's mind reeled, and she couldn't convince herself this was reality. A whispering sigh escaped her as Rand buried his face along the side of her neck, his mouth spreading hot kisses over her naked flesh. Karen caught her breath at the flood of pleasure, her fingers gripping his head, drawing him back to her lips. His open mouth sought hers in an urgent kiss that sent her world careening. His hands, sensuously caressing her hip, slipped upward, capturing the ripe fullness of her upturned breast, and she was swept along in a violent whirlpool of desire. Winding her arms around his back and pressing her full length to him, she answered his passion with her own.

Suddenly, Rand tensed, his muscles rigid with attention. Lifting his head, he listened attentively to the stillness, leaving her naked and bereft as he stood in anticipation.

"Rand?" Karen whispered, sitting upright.

"I thought I heard a noise." Wearily, he rubbed his hands over his face. He lowered himself onto the bed; leaning forward, he buried his face in his hands.

"I thought you'd gone." She covered herself with the housecoat from the end of the bed.

He smiled wryly. "I couldn't find my coat. What happened in here?"

She gestured weakly with her hand. "I was crying and didn't see where I was going."

He nodded, his face weary and pinched.

"Please, Rand," she pleaded, her voice wobbling dangerously, "don't do this to us."

He stiffened at the sound of her voice. "Don't…it's over."

"There will never be anyone who will love you as much as I do." Bitterness was etched in her pain-ridden eyes.

He stood abruptly, hurrying from her room. "I've got to get out of here. Damn it, Karen, my coat."

Tying the sash of her housecoat, she followed him into the living room and to the closet.

"Here." She handed it to him. "I'm going to let you go, and I'm not even going to say good-bye. We'll probably never meet again. You'll live your life, and I'll live mine. But I love you, Rand. I'll love you as long as I live, and some-day, maybe not for a long time, you'll regret this."

The hand closed over the door handle was

clenched so tight it became stark white. He didn't pause or acknowledge her words. Instead, he yanked open the door and left.

Karen jerked as the door slammed, crying as she had never cried, her breath coming in desperate gasps, the tears from her soul.

Hugging her arms protectively against her stomach, she sat in the chair Rand had vacated, curling into its softness like a hurt child seeking comfort from a parent. The gold locket and bracelet remained on the floor, and Karen stared at the glimmering gold for a long time before bending down to retrieve the pair. Clenching them to her breast, she rocked back and forth with an anguish too deep for tears.

She remained in the chair the entire night, her gaze watching the candles while they burned themselves out. First one, then the other, the last desperate flicker before extinction. The room went dark. Karen stared with sightless eyes into a moonlit, shadow-filled room, realizing the throbbing pain in her head would diminish, but not the pain in her heart.

The sun, gradually rising to announce a new day, spurred her into sluggish action. It took a careful application of makeup to camouflage the red swollen eyes as she dressed for work. "I'll make it through this day, and then I'll be all right," she told herself, knowing she was lying. It would be a very long time before she was all right again.

Until that day, Karen had had no idea how good she was at lying, how automatic certain responses became in one's life.

Late afternoon, she sat at her desk, examining the final details of a day's work, knowing she'd never find solace in her job, wondering if she'd ever find comfort.

Matthew's cheerful face was waiting for her outside her apartment. Karen avoided his eyes, praying he wouldn't mention Rand.

"Evening, lass."

"Hi, Dad. I'm kinda busy..." She didn't have the heart to tell him he couldn't come inside.

"'Tis fine. I'll only stay a minute." He followed her and sat at the kitchen table while she put on coffee to brew. When she gave him a sidelong glance, she found he was watching her with an odd expression.

"When will ye be seeing Rand again?"

Karen turned back to the countertop, closing her eyes for a moment at the searing pain. "I won't," she said flatly.

She could sense the shock that rocked him. "I'm sure I must not be hearing ye right," he said after a few minutes of stunned shock.

"Look, Dad"—her voice shook violently— "I don't feel much like discussing it right now."

"But ye love him," he cried indignantly.

"Of course I love him," she whispered through the pain.

"And he loves you?" This time, Matthew's voice was quiet and probing.

Karen couldn't keep her bottom lip from trembling. "Yes, he loves me…but love doesn't make everything right," she uttered in a hoarse whisper, blinking wildly to restrain the tears.

"But why?" her father asked in confusion. It was a question that had haunted Karen half the night.

"Because he's proud; he thinks he's only half a man and if I love him now, that love will eventually die when he loses his eyesight completely." She inhaled a shaky breath. "He wants me so much it's eating a hole in him; he had to push me away before it was too late." Karen grimaced with the memory that she had accused Rand of being half a man, lashing back where it would hurt him the most because he was hurting her so desperately.

Gently, a pair of hands settled on her shoulders and turned her around.

"Don't," she told him tautly, shrugging off his hands. "I'm a grown woman now. I'm not your little girl anymore."

Matthew ignored her, turning her into his arms, holding her close, his cheek resting gently against her head. "Even big girls require a father's comfort every now and then," he whispered.

Karen buried her head against his chest, the tension draining from her as she allowed the tears to come. "Oh, Dad, I love him so much."

"I know you do, lass," Matthew crooned. "Let it all out, darlin'. Let it all out."

A week passed. Matthew and Judy enfolded Karen in their love and support, trying to make sure she was busy, not letting her stay alone for any long length of time. Karen lost weight she could ill afford to lose, and her eyes developed dark shadows that cosmetics were unable to hide. When she wasn't working or with her family, she sat in the big overstuffed chair, looking pensive and lost.

Matthew seemed to feel talking about Rand would make things easier. Her father felt certain that once Rand had come to his senses, he would be back. Karen didn't bother to correct him.

Another week slipped by, and Karen knew she couldn't live like this much longer. Friday afternoon, she gave Tacoma Cable a two-week notice, drove home, and handed a similar notice to the apartment manager.

"Lass." Her father let himself into her apartment, his face hurt and confused. "What have ye done?"

Karen didn't pause. "I'm leaving Tacoma," she announced without emotion. Dark curls escaped the scarf she'd tied around her head. She was standing on the kitchen counter, cleaning out her top cupboards. Boxes littered both the kitchen and the living-room floor. "I should have done this two weeks ago." She dipped the cleaning rag in the bucket of hot, steaming water and wrung it out.

"But, lass, when Rand comes back…"

"Dad," she protested angrily, "when will you get it into your thick skull? Rand isn't going to come back. It's over between us."

Matthew grew visibly pale and sat down.

"Dad"—concern laced her voice, and she jumped down from the counter—"are you all right?"

He nodded weakly. "I'm fine." His eyes searched hers, holding a desperate appeal. "I don't want you doing something rash. You've been hurt, and seeking a geographical cure would be the worst possible thing for you. I told you before, things have a way of working out for the best. Just where are ye planning to go?"

Karen had expected an argument, and squared her shoulders defiantly. "Away…I don't know yet."

Matthew shook his head sadly. "I don't like this, lass."

Karen had known he wouldn't and that she hadn't heard the last of it. "I'm twenty-four years old, and I've barely left the state of Washington. I think it's time I learned to live a little, let my hair down, travel." Her enthusiasm was as phony as that of a used-car salesman. There was only one thing she wanted in life, and that was impossible. She couldn't chance meeting Rand. She couldn't stay. Not in the same city, not in the same state. Not in the same world.

Judy arrived an hour later; her eyes held an accusing, disbelieving look. "You've pulled some good ones in your life, little sister, but this takes the cake."

"Oh? What have I done now?"

"Do you realize you've got Dad worried sick?"

Karen flushed guiltily, dropping the pretense. "I know, but I've got to leave. I wish I could make you understand. Do you realize what it does to me every time I'm near the university or see Uncle Evan or even drive in downtown Tacoma? Someday it's going to happen. By fate or design, I don't know, but someday I'm going to run into Rand. I won't be able to take it." Her voice rose, and she took a moment to compose herself. "I'll fall into a thousand pieces. I know

I will. If you and Dad think I'm running away, then all right, I'll admit it."

Judy sighed, her eyes filled with compassion. "I wish I had some magic formula that would take away the hurt, but I don't." She gave a weak gesture of helplessness. "I'm not convinced you're doing the wrong thing, like Dad is. But I do know we all love you. Let our love support you; let us be your strength." She paused for a minute and withdrew something from her purse. "Maybe if you read this, it'll help."

Karen accepted the letter, grown yellow with age.

"When Mom died," Judy continued, "Mike and I were stationed back East. Both boys were little, and I was stuck home alone most of the time. I had no family, no close friends, or anyone I could talk to about my feelings. I didn't know how to handle my grief. For weeks, I walked around in a haze of emotional pain."

Karen understood; her life had been a haze of pain since that last night with Rand.

"All I seemed capable of doing was crying. I know Mike was worried about me. He must have written Dad because I received this letter. It's the most beautiful thing Dad has ever given me."

Karen opened the letter and was greeted by Matthew's familiar scrawl. The date was exactly three months after her mother's death. It was a vivid memory. Madeline had suffered from a chronic kidney disorder, and when she contracted an infection, it didn't overly concern Karen or her father. She'd had several infections over the years. Karen had even felt her mother was getting better. Then one day she was in the hospital, insisting she should be home, and two days later she was dead.

Karen had loved and sorely missed her mother, too, but her concern had been for Matthew and the changes that had come over him after Madeline's death.

The letter showed the wear of many readings; the stain of Judy's tears marked the pages.

It read:

My darling Judy,
It hurts so terribly, doesn't it? But, my darling lass, we must learn to accept the pain. It is the price we must pay for having loved. I hold this ache of loneliness inside, and although I have loved and lost my beloved Madeline, I accept and gladly pay the cost. It is but a small price for the love we shared those many years. They have been good years, the best of my life. Sometimes I am overcome by my agony. I weep with you,

my daughter. I pray God will surround you with His love.

Mike is worried about you. He loves you just as I loved my Madeline. Drink of his love; let it be your strength.

We must go on, just as life does. James and Carter need you just as Karen yet needs me. Accept the pain with joy…it was worth the cost.

Your loving father

Tears blurred Karen's eyes and spilled down her face. The end of her relationship with Rand was very much like her mother's death to Judy. She smiled through her tears, grateful for her sister's love. She, too, would pay the price for loving Rand, but now, because of a letter full of love and wisdom, she would pay the price with joy.

Judy may have accepted Karen's decision to leave, but Matthew made repeated efforts to dissuade her. Karen listened politely to his logic, sometimes doubting the wisdom of her actions, but never wavering from the decision.

Selling her furniture and packing her things filled her last remaining days in Tacoma. It was the nights that continued to haunt her. She'd lay awake for hours in a reflective mood, wondering what she might have done differently to have won Rand. The sharp pain remained, and Karen pondered how long it would take for it to lessen. Sometimes, if she lay very still and closed her eyes, she could almost feel the warmth of his breath against her cheek. She'd shake herself, realizing she was doing the right thing by leaving. She couldn't bear the struggle to be free of him for much longer. All the memories were right here to torment her.

Only three days remained of Karen's two-week notice. Most of the things from her apartment had been sold. Only her bed and the large, overstuffed chair remained.

Because she couldn't sleep, she sat reading, finding it hard to concentrate and equally difficult to answer the doubts that bobbed to the surface of her mind. Karen realized, perhaps for the first time, how much she would miss her home, her city. If she were honest with herself, she'd admit that she didn't really want to leave Tacoma, but the alternative was just as unacceptable.

When the doorbell rang, it caught Karen by surprise. She glanced at her watch, curious who would be visiting so late.

"Who is it?" she questioned before unlocking the door.

"Rand," came the muffled reply.

Was it some cruel joke? Her fingers were trembling so badly she could barely open the door.

When he entered, Karen was as shocked by his appearance as his presence. He looked as if he hadn't shaved in days; the dark growth did little to disguise his haggard features. Gaunt lines of fatigue were etched about his eyes and mouth, as if he hadn't seen a bed in days. If he had slept, it was in the wrinkled mass of clothes he wore. His hair, normally so neat and well groomed, looked like he'd raked his fingers through it several times over.

"Rand?" His name was twisted from her in shock. She longed to touch him, to comfort him. He was in as much hell as she had been these past weeks.

His mouth twisted cynically. "All right, Karen, you win."

Seven

Karen walked into his arms, gently resting her head against his chest. His hold tightened until it was difficult for her to breathe. But it didn't matter, not as long as she was in his arms. Rand's face moved against her hair, as if he couldn't yet believe the feel of her. They stood entwined for a long time, not talking, hardly breathing, savoring the tender moment.

When Karen placed her arms around his neck, urging his mouth to hers, she felt his reluctance. The kiss began hard, as if he wanted to punish her; then, with a groan, his lips softened into a warm possession, and what followed was anything but punishment.

"Hold me, please, hold me." Tears blurred her vision, her voice betraying the anguish of the past month without him.

"I love you." His voice was thick with emotion as if he were confessing a guilt. "I could have withstood anything if I didn't love you so much."

"I know, I know," she whispered in soothing tones, remembering how hard he had tried to convince her otherwise. Tenderly, his hand brushed her tears aside. "I think I would have died if you hadn't come," Karen murmured. Already she had gone cold inside, withdrawing from her family and life.

Rand breathed heavily. "I'm here now." The words were clipped, almost angry.

His pride made him so defensive, Karen thought sadly. Knowing and loving Rand made her realize how much it had cost him to come to her.

"There's only one chair left in the apartment." She gave a tiny laugh and wiped the last happy tears from her face. "I'll have to sit on your lap."

The quizzical look on his face prompted her to add, "Everything else has been sold. I'm packed and ready to leave." Her arms automatically went around his neck as she positioned herself on his knees.

His hands tightened around her upper arms. "Were you so sure of me?" His look was weary, and there was a grimness in him.

"I wasn't sure of anything," she said, defending herself. Her eyes narrowed questioningly. Certainly he couldn't believe she had expected his return. In truth, she had never been more shocked in her life.

"I want the wedding to be small." The demand startled Karen. She hadn't expected him to mention marriage, not yet. Not that it mattered how many guests attended.

"Wedding?" Karen breathed in wonder as her heart soared with a new happiness. She began spreading kisses over his face, and fresh tears misted her eyes.

"Your father wouldn't accept anything less," Rand murmured caustically. "Nor would you."

Karen was too happy to question his decision.

They were married nine days later in Evan and Milly Forsyth's home. The preceding days were a whirlwind of activity as Judy, Karen, and her godmother rushed to have everything ready. Karen saw Rand only once, when they applied for their wedding license, and if he was curt and taciturn, she attributed it to nerves and the pressures of teaching. Because Rand had a speaking engagement in New York scheduled for the weekend of their wedding, it was decided that Karen would travel with him on a working honeymoon. Rand's mother lived in New York, and Karen was eager to meet her.

As Rand wished, the wedding was unpretentious, with only family and a few intimate friends attending. The Forsyth home was decorated with garlands and several bouquets of fresh flowers. Their sweet fragrance lingered in the air, their colors vivid. Karen felt she couldn't have asked for a more lovely wedding.

As Randall Franklin Prescott and Karen Madeline McAlister exchanged their vows, Rand's voice was firm and unfaltering. Karen's voice trembled slightly as she repeated hers. Her heart swelled with a burning love. Marrying Rand was the culmination of every romantic dream she'd ever had.

The wedding meal was served in the Forsyths' huge dining room. If Rand was somber and unusually quiet, no one noticed, for Karen was so obviously happy. Her spirits soared with an unrestrained freedom, yet she had just uttered vows that bound her for life.

It was late by the time they arrived at Rand's home. The stars were out in an ostentatious show, their brilliance lighting up the black velvet sky.

As Carl carried in her cases, Karen looped her arm in Rand's, savoring the beauty of the evening. "This reminds me of the night we met." She smiled dreamily, placing her head against his upper arm. "Oh, Rand, I'm so happy...I love you so much." She longed to have him take her in his arms and whisk her over the threshold, but he paused, holding himself stiff and unyielding against her.

"My mother had a homemade sampler in the living room when I was a little girl. I've thought about it so often these past few days. I'd like to make one for our home."

Rand remained unresponsive, and Karen hugged herself to him. "Aren't you interested in what it said?" she asked with a gentle smile.

"I have the feeling you're going to tell me whether I want to hear it or not," he murmured.

Karen laughed. "It said, 'If you love something, set it free. If it doesn't return, it was never meant to be. But if it does, love it forever.'" She gave a long sigh. "I let you go that night. It nearly killed me to let you walk out of my life, but you've come back, and now I'll love you forever."

Rand jerked her arm from his. "That's just the point," he retorted angrily. "I didn't come back. You forced me into this farce."

"Forced you?" Karen asked in confusion. "I *didn't* show up on *your* doorstep. You were the one who came to me."

Rand gave a short, derisive laugh. "That I did, two hours before the deadline." He stormed into the house, leaving Karen standing alone and baffled. When she followed him, Rand had already poured himself a tall drink from a decanter of whiskey.

"I thought you said you rarely drink?" she asked accusingly.

He snickered. "I find I can't stand to be in your presence without something to dull my sense of decency."

"That's a rotten thing to say." What was happening to him? Why was he acting like this? Karen searched his face, hoping to find some clue of what was wrong. All she could read was contempt.

"That'll be all, Carl." Rand broke into her thoughts. "I'll call you when we're ready to leave for the airport."

Carl's eyes avoided Karen's, although she silently pleaded with him; for what, she didn't know.

As soon as the front door closed behind her husband's driver, Karen asked, "What…what did you mean when you said you came to me two hours before the deadline? What deadline?"

His face twisted malevolently. "Drop the charade, Karen. You're not going to fool me by playing dumb. I'd guessed you'd try something like this."

"Something like what? Rand, please, I don't know what you're talking about."

He emitted another sadistic laugh. "I walked

into the whole thing like a lamb going to the slaughter. I have to admire you, Karen. You were more cunning than I thought possible."

"Rand?" she pleaded urgently. "I don't know what you're talking about."

"Sure you don't." He tipped his head back and drained the glass. "I needed that." Wiping his mouth with the back of his hand, he sat, leaning his head against the back of the couch. "Like a lamb to the slaughter," he repeated. "You must have been frantic when you saw your little ploy wouldn't work that night. You hadn't counted on me handing you your walking papers so soon, did you? It was quick thinking on your part to pretend you'd hurt yourself. It got me into that bedroom." He ran his hand over his eyes. "I should have known something was up when you were practically naked."

"I'd spilled wine on my dress," she cried.

"Sure you did." His words were uttered in a harsh whisper.

Karen paced the living-room floor, her mind racing, her thoughts confused. Nothing made sense, least of all the things he was saying. "Rand," she whispered imploringly, "I'm going to ask you one last time. Please tell me what's going on."

He sat upright, flexing his shoulders as if he were going to ignore her. "What did you expect me to do? Welcome you with open arms? I don't take kindly to blackmail; I could hate you and your father for what you've done to me."

"Blackmail? Dad?" She glared at him, her face tightening with shock. Walking the full length of the floor, Karen poured herself a drink from the same decanter Rand had used, then choked and coughed after the first gulp. "Good grief, how do you drink this stuff?" Her eyes were watering, and she shook her head; her mouth felt as if she'd been sucking lemons. She moved back to Rand. "All right," she murmured tightly, "let's start at the beginning. I invited you to dinner—"

"Like a black widow to her web," Rand interrupted mockingly.

Karen clenched her hands together, fighting the urge to scream. "I invited you to dinner because…because I had to know what was happening with us."

"Ha!" Rand laughed sarcastically. "More likely to lure me to your bed so your father could find us."

"So my father could find us?" She echoed one of the short, bitter laughs he'd given her. "Really, Rand, if I'd gotten you into my bed, the last person I'd want to see is my father."

"So you say," he remarked flippantly.

Karen studied him closely again, feeling hurt and bewildered.

"I have to admit your duplicity worked well. I wasn't given much choice, was I? Since Evan Forsyth is your godfather, who do you think he'd believe?" His mouth twisted bitterly. "I haven't got ten years in at the university; you knew that. I'd stand a snowball's chance in hell of finding another decent position after Forsyth was through with me."

Even as understanding came, Karen refused to believe what she was hearing. Matthew had seen them together that night and was using what he'd witnessed against Rand, forcing him to marry her. She inhaled sharply. "The noise that night was Dad," she said incredulously, her voice tight with embarrassment.

"My contempt would be less if you'd admit your part in this."

"Damn it, Rand," she shouted, "I *am* telling you the truth." Suddenly, her knees became so weak she had to sit down. She sat tense and stiff in the chair opposite Rand as she pleaded with him. "Please listen to me." She spoke softly, enunciating each word. "I swear by everything I hold sacred that I had nothing to do with this."

Uncertainty flashed across his face, wrinkling his brow. "I could almost believe you... almost." His fingers twisted the wedding band, so recently placed on his finger, tying him to her. "But everything falls into place so neatly. You set up this trap for me..."

"I didn't, I swear," she cried.

"All right, you didn't, but why was it when I came to your room, thinking you were hurt, that I found you half-naked?"

"I already explained that," she pleaded. "I spilled wine on my dress. I had to take it off and soak it, or it would have been ruined. After I removed the dress, I bumped into the closet door."

"Your father just happened to walk in and witness that sordid little scene with us on the floor?"

Karen felt sick. "Dad...Dad has a terrible habit of walking into my apartment unannounced."

Rand's face turned sour. "Sure he does. You were so confident you had me trapped that you quit your job and packed your things."

"No! I'd decided to leave Tacoma...to move away." Karen could see it was useless; she couldn't argue or reason with him. Rand had already tried her and found her guilty. "Nothing I can say will make a difference, will it?"

"That's right," he jeered. "I have to admit you play the innocent well, but I've fallen for your deceit once. I won't be such easy prey next time."

A sick sensation churned her stomach; they could never build a marriage under the circumstances. "I realize you believe I was involved in this. I think I can even understand that." She spoke softly, her voice barely audible. "The evidence certainly points in that direction."

"What takes the cake is that you even had the marriage performed at the Forsyth home," he accused her again. "That was like rubbing salt in an open wound, my dear."

"That's the point, isn't it?" she asked, with pain-filled eyes. "I'm not your dear. You must hate me." Karen didn't know how she could sound so calm when she wanted to scream.

Rand's fingers tightened around the whiskey glass until Karen was sure the tumbler would be crushed into a thousand pieces. "I wish I could hate you," he whispered in a tone that reminded her of the night he'd returned and admitted his love almost as if it were a guilty secret.

"You once reminded me that we are two adults," she began shakily, gathering her resolve, "and that we should be able to handle things in an adult manner."

Rand nodded curtly.

"I can only apologize for my father's behavior. I don't know why he would do something so underhanded…"

"Karen…" Rand's voice rose threateningly.

Despondently, Karen realized Rand thought she was placing the blame entirely on Matthew's head.

"Please, let me finish," she asked, her voice stiff, polite. "I can only hope that someday you'll find it in your heart to forgive Dad… and to think kindly of me." She slipped the exquisite diamond from her long, slender finger and watched it slide off with a sadness she had never known. The ring had been on her finger for only a few hours, and Karen thought she'd rather have lost her finger than part with this symbol of their love. "I'm…I'm giving you the wedding ring back. I'll begin annulment proceedings first thing Monday morning."

Rand smiled stiffly as he accepted the diamond. "Maybe an annulment would be best."

"I'll have my things moved out before you return from New York," she said weakly, fighting back the first shock waves.

Rand's look became intent. "Where will you go?"

She turned away from him, tilting her head back and blinking wildly to keep the tears from spilling. "I…I don't know yet, but it won't matter. Once the annulment is final…" She left the rest unsaid, the words stuck in her throat.

Rand slouched forward, running his fingers through his hair. "You don't need to leave immediately. I'll be gone for the next three days. We both need time to think, to decide what we're going to do. By the time I return, I'll have the situation in perspective and a better grip on my emotions. I think you should do the same thing. We'll talk then. Is that agreeable?"

"All right," she murmured tightly. "I'll stay here for now and let my family assume I've left for New York with you. Maybe while you're gone, I'll come up with a solution to this mess."

"Until we decide, I'd like for you to keep the ring."

Miserably, Karen shook her head. "No...I don't think I should. Marriage is something very binding as far as I'm concerned. My parents were married for twenty-seven years, and if I place a wedding ring on my finger, I think my intention should be for a lifetime...not a three-day weekend."

Rand frowned slightly. "Whether we stay married or not, the ring is yours."

"I'd prefer it if you kept it for now." The ring would become very much like the bracelet he'd given her. Unless they stayed married, it could be only a painful reminder of what could have been.

Carl drove Rand to the airport an hour later. If he was surprised that Karen was staying behind, he didn't show it. Sadly, Karen stood in the open doorway as the car drove into the distance, watching until the lights faded and the car turned onto the main road. Rand's farewell had been cool, but the open hostility was gone. For that, at least, Karen could be grateful. Rand's face was drawn and tired as he'd stepped into the car, and Karen yearned to go to him and erase the finely strung tension between them. But she'd stayed where she was, watching him go.

Her suitcase remained in the master bedroom, a room indelibly marked by Rand's presence, and Karen avoided it as long as possible. Instead, she sat in the sunken living room, feeling lost and very much alone. Suddenly, she remembered this was her wedding night and could have wept with bitterness and disappointment.

Shortly after midnight, it began to rain, a steady torrent with mounting fury that pounded sheets of rain against the windows. Thunder rolled closer and closer; lightning flashed in jagged arcs across the sky. How quickly the storm had come; only a few hours before, Karen had been staring at clear skies and brilliant stars. The storm was like the day. It had begun with such promise; she had entered Rand's home as his wife, determined to do her best. Now, only a few hours later, her marriage was threatened, her life in turmoil.

When the phone rang, Karen was surprised. "Hello," she answered hesitantly. Surely Rand didn't receive many calls after midnight. More than likely it was a prank call.

"Miss Karen?"

The voice was familiar, and Karen recognized it immediately. "Yes, Carl, it's me."

He sounded awkward, as if he didn't often use the telephone. "I was phoning to see if you are all right…the storm and all."

"I'm fine, thank you. I'm not frightened by thunder and lightning. Did…did Rand get off okay?"

"I assume he and Miss Dibner were not delayed. I didn't stay to see the flight off."

Cora was with Rand. A sick feeling came over Karen's stomach. She had endured so much this day, the whole gauntlet of emotions from utter happiness to abject misery. Knowing Cora was traveling with Rand was almost more than she could bear.

"No, of course you wouldn't wait to see him off," Karen murmured, the lump in her throat building. "Thank you for your concern, Carl, but I'm fine."

"Let me know if you need anything," he offered soberly.

"I will." Her voice suddenly sounded frail and wobbly.

There was a pause on the other end of the line. "Good night, then."

"Good night." She replaced the receiver, looking around her helplessly. Rand and Cora. The picture of them traveling together when it was her and Rand's wedding night was almost more than she could bear. When the sobs came, she roughly jerked her hand across her face. If this was what love does, Karen decided, she wanted no part of it.

Stiffening her back, she turned out the living-room lights and walked determinedly into the master bedroom. Ignoring Rand's dominating presence, marked in every corner, she lifted her suitcase onto the king-size bed and took out her nightgown. It was a lovely full-length satin of pale blue that Judy had given her before the wedding. Karen took one look at it, stuffed it back inside the suitcase, and slammed the lid closed. Randall Prescott could fly across the country with another woman on their wedding night, but she…but she… The anger drained as quickly as it had flared.

Karen sat on the bed and lightly ran her fingers along the pattern of the multi-brown-colored bedspread. For an instant, she'd been ready to run, to surrender without so much as a confrontation. She couldn't stay, yet she couldn't leave. Releasing her breath slowly, Karen wandered from the room and found two other large-size bedrooms and a den that Rand obviously used as an office. She moved her suitcase into one of the other bedrooms; sleeping in the master bedroom was an agony she couldn't bear tonight.

Karen woke early the next morning, her heart heavy. She sat up, deciding to get away from the house for a while and sort through her thoughts. Evidence of the night's storm littered the yard; short branches of fir and pine from the trees that surrounded the property were scattered everywhere. Karen kicked them aside, her irritation so strong she failed to appreciate the freshness of the early-morning air. Heavy gray clouds continued to darken the sky, rain ready to pelt the earth at any time. Yet Karen noticed none of this.

"Just wait till I get my hands on you, Dad," she said aloud, letting the branches receive the brunt of her anger.

Did her father realize the impossible position he had put her in? What could he possibly have been thinking? Blackmailing Rand was an underhanded trick that went against the very core of honesty she had always known from her father. Karen wanted to shout at him every rotten name she knew. How could he have possibly done anything so unscrupulous? Rand had every reason to detest the backhanded methods Matthew had used to get them married. And yet as much as she disagreed with her father's schemes, she could understand why he did it. Against the flint hardness of his will, against his better judgment, Rand loved her. But that love was doomed almost from the beginning. Without Matthew's intervention, there would never have been a marriage. Now it was up to Karen to see that they remained married. With a new resolve, she walked back to the house.

A movement out of the corner of her eyes caught her attention, and she found Carl watching her from the kitchen of his home. Impulsively, she gave him a friendly wave and watched the smile grow on his face before he returned her greeting.

"Miss Karen."

She turned to find Carl's long strides eliminating the space between them. The calico kitten James and Carter had given Rand was under his arm.

"Hello, Number Nine," she greeted the kitten softly. She was more cat than kitten, and Karen was surprised how much she had grown. "I wondered what had become of you."

"Mr. Rand asked the missus and me to keep the kitty while he was away, but…"

"I'll take her," Karen offered, interrupting him to avoid explanations of why she was here and Rand in New York.

Carl handed her the cat. "With Mr. Rand gone so much of the time, the kitty seems to think of my place as home. The missus has tried to discourage her, but she stands outside the kitchen door and cries until we let her inside. My missus has a soft heart," he added.

Karen concealed a smile. No doubt Dorothy was a warmhearted soul, but it didn't take Karen long to realize Carl had a soft touch where animals were concerned. She'd found hay, food, and a salt block by the creek and knew he'd hauled it down the narrow path to feed the wild creatures in the woods.

"Now that I'm here, Number Nine will know her home," Karen said, her voice conveying the confidence of her newly formed resolve. "She's had her shots and everything?" Rand was sure to want her spayed as soon as possible.

"Oh, yes. First thing Mr. Rand had me do was take her to the vet."

"Thank you, Carl." The older man was fast becoming both ally and friend. Karen was grateful for both.

Without hesitation, Karen entered her new

home, walking straight to the master bedroom. The cat followed her, jumped on the king-size bed, and curled into a little ball as if that were exactly where she belonged. *I'll do the same,* Karen decided.

One side of Rand's walk-in closet had been cleared for her things, and Karen spent the rest of the morning unpacking. She found herself singing, her confidence building. As she placed her things around the room, a sense of rightness replaced her insecurities. If her father could convince her mother to marry him, certainly she should be able to persuade Rand, who she knew loved her, that they should stay married. She'd face him with that quiet, unshakable McAlister resolve, she decided. Feeling as if a weight had been lifted from her, Karen slept in the master bedroom that night, finding courage in the fact that she was acting like a wife, waiting for her husband's return.

Rand's flight was due late Sunday afternoon. Karen waited impatiently as each minute passed with an incredible slowness. After pacing the floor innumerable times and checking the dinner she'd cooked, Karen decided she needed to vent some of her anxiety by walking.

She followed the same path she'd discovered the day before, a winding trail that led into tall trees alive with a natural beauty. When she returned, strolling leisurely into the clearing beside the house, she saw Carl's car had returned and was parked in front. Her footsteps hastened, her long strides filled with purpose.

"Hello, Carl," she called happily.

He gave her a frown that confused her and stepped into the entryway carrying Rand's suitcase. "I'll be heading home to *my missus,*" Carl quipped, his tone showing obvious displeasure.

He tipped his cap to Karen, his eyes avoiding hers. As Karen watched him go, her eyes clouded with confusion. Stopping to take a deep breath, she entered the house, but the welcoming smile died on her lips as soon as she moved through the door.

"Darling," Cora purred, her arms entwined around Rand's neck. "She must have left."

Eight

"But I haven't," Karen interrupted, fighting to keep her voice even and to hide her shock.

Gripping Cora's wrists, Rand forcefully removed her hands, which continued to cling to him. "Karen, I…" He sounded unsure and disconcerted.

"You must be exhausted from the flight, Cora," Karen interrupted again. If Rand wanted to give her an explanation, he could do it later, privately. "I'll have Carl drive you home." She returned Cora's cold glare with one of her own. Cora may have found encouragement in the fact that Rand had left her on their wedding night, but the woman had yet to discover the lengths Karen was willing to go to keep her husband.

Carl must have been waiting outside, because the minute his name was mentioned, he entered the house. "I'm ready to leave, Miss Dibner."

He gave Karen a conspiratorial wink that did little to please Cora.

"Rand," she purred, giving the impression her feelings had been crushed by such a lack of welcome. But if she'd hoped for his support, she was again disappointed.

"As Karen says, you must be tired from the flight. I know I am."

"You will phone me?" Cora's attitude immediately changed from a feline on the prowl to the businesswoman she was. Professionally, Cora was Rand's equal, her list of credentials as impressive as Rand's. The look she flashed Karen let her know she had yet to concede the battle.

"I'll contact you in the morning," Rand murmured without enthusiasm.

Her eyes filled with resentment; she gave Karen an almost imperceptible nod.

Karen returned with a slight dip of her head. "We'll meet again. Goodbye, Cora."

With a cool sophistication Karen envied, Cora gave her a meaningful sidelong glare on her way out the door. "You can count on it," she murmured for Karen's ears alone.

As soon as the door was closed, Rand crossed the living room and poured himself a stiff drink from the whiskey decanter. "I didn't mean for that to happen," he began, but his voice contained no apology, his posture defensive.

"I'm sure you didn't," Karen murmured.

"Where were you?" he demanded. "I walked in the door expecting you to be here."

For the first time since his arrival, Karen began to relax. "I went for a walk in the woods out back. I wasn't exactly sure what time you planned on being here."

His face showed fatigue. "Did you discover the creek?" he questioned, then took a sip of his drink.

"Yes, I did." She was still standing in the same spot as when she'd come in.

"Carl has seen several deer drinking from it. I believe he's put some hay and a salt block out for them."

"I wondered about that," Karen said stiffly. Why did they have to talk to each other like polite strangers? Why couldn't they come to the matter that was uppermost in both their minds?

"Would you like something to eat?"

He shook his head dismissively. "I ate on the plane."

"Yes…of course you would." She glanced at the meal simmering in the kitchen, feeling chagrined. He was three hours ahead of the West Coast, and by his clock it was nearly eight. He would have eaten long ago.

Rand lifted his head and turned his face toward the kitchen. "You've cooked dinner?"

"I didn't go to any trouble; it's nothing special." She dismissed his concern and walked into the kitchen to turn off the oven. She had no appetite, and wouldn't until things were cleared between them.

He followed her, wrinkling his nose appreciatively. "What's this nothing special you're cooking?"

Placing a rebelling curl of soft brown hair around her ear, she turned her back to the stove. "Cornish game hens in orange sauce."

The beginnings of a smile threatened his stiff mouth. "If you consider this nothing, I'll look forward to your fancy meals."

She gave a small, nervous laugh. "Actually, I'm not a very good cook. I thought I'd ask Dorothy if she'd share some of her recipes."

"It was a very wifely thing to have dinner waiting for me."

Did she imagine an inquiry in his voice? If so, she wasn't likely to ignore it. "Yes, it was," she said as matter-of-factly as possible. "I…I am your wife, for the present, at least."

Rand scowled, and Karen's heart sank. She couldn't stand it for another minute. If he wasn't going to say something, she would. "I think the question remains of exactly how long I am to be your wife."

A muscle flexed in his jaw, and Karen could

see the pride that narrowed his eyes. "Yes, that does seem to be the question. What have you decided?"

For a moment, Karen's stomach pitched unsteadily. Her hands twisted together, and she looked around, wondering why she had to have the most important discussion of her life in a kitchen with her back supported by an oven door because she was too nervous to stand upright.

"I've decided that my father played a dirty trick on the both of us. I know you believe I had a hand in this scheme, but I didn't."

Rand's mouth twisted.

"I know you don't believe me," she continued, her voice shaky. "Someday, I pray, you'll trust me enough to accept what I'm telling you as the truth. I do know"—she hesitated, her voice dipping slightly—"that I'm glad Dad did what he did. Admittedly, it was an underhanded trick, unworthy of my father, but you would never have married me otherwise, and Dad knew it."

"You knew that, too," he said tightly, accusingly.

"I only know you love me and that it hurt you just as much as it did me to walk away that night. I know that you'll never hold another woman in your arms without pretending it's me. I know that if you send me away, you'll always wonder about the life we could have had together."

"I never said I loved you." His upper lip curled into a defensive smile.

Karen's response was gentle. "You did the night you came back, the night of the deadline. But it doesn't matter if you spoke the words or not. I would have known, anyway. I've known for a long time. Do you imagine you could have hidden it from me the night we walked along Commencement Bay? Or any number of times since when you've held me in your arms?"

Ominously, Rand's jaw tightened. His fingers raked his hair in a savage motion. "All right, I love you, but it doesn't change things." The words were hardly an admission of tenderness, but more a biting accusation.

She met his fury calmly. "The only thing left to decide is the status of our relationship. Are we going to stay married, or are you going to allow that arrogant pride of yours to ruin both our lives?"

Karen could actually witness the inner turmoil etched so painfully on his profile. "No, we're married now. God knows it's not what I wanted for either of us, but the deed is done, and I haven't the strength to undo it."

"Okay," she whispered on a lengthy, drawn-out breath. Her love-filled eyes searched his face.

"All I know is I can't bear to face life without you now. I can't let you go again. It hurt too damn much the first time."

"I know," she said, assuring him of her own pain. Still, they remained apart at opposite ends of the kitchen. "Will you meet me halfway, Rand?"

His face relaxed, his look almost tender.

They walked into each other's arms, their grip tightening as if they never wanted to part again. When his mouth found hers, it was a gentle kiss that soon deepened. Karen's body flooded with warm excitement, and she moved against him sensuously, her arms locked around his neck.

No matter how deep their desire had run before, Karen had always tasted Rand's restraint. Now he returned his love and physical appetite in full. Their needs rose to a fever pitch; his kisses left her panting and breathless.

"I find I'm hungry," he whispered huskily against her ear. "I'm starving to death, but my want is not for food."

Karen gave a demure laugh, his words touching a spark of urgency within her. Tears of happiness glistened in her dark eyes as she spread happy kisses over his face. "Then let us wait no longer to dine."

Gathering her close, he kissed her brow and then her lips longingly, smiling down on her. "Yes, let us wait no longer to dine." He kissed her again, and her mouth parted in welcome. Again and again, their mouths met, each kiss more ardent, more rousing.

A soft sigh escaped Karen as she laid her head on his chest. His fingers brushed the soft curls from her neck, clearing the way for his lips.

Karen nestled against him, curving her womanly figure all the closer. "Will you carry me over the threshold?"

She could feel the smile against the satin smoothness of her neck. "It's raining outside."

"I meant the threshold of our bedroom," she whispered.

Rand groaned; their lips met again, rousing Karen until she gave a deep, heaving sigh of longing.

His hands caressed her back, sliding over her hips and buttocks, pressing her softness against his solid length. Bending slightly, he placed his arm behind her knees and lifted her from the floor. Her arms automatically went around his neck, and she rested her head on his shoulder. The tip of her tongue found the sensitive area behind his ear. When he gave a muted groan, she turned her attention to the thick column of his neck, spreading delicate kisses there until he shuddered.

A whisper of a sigh escaped her as Rand placed her with infinite care on their bed.

"Wait," she pleaded breathlessly.

"Wait?"

She thrilled to the impatience in his voice. "I'll be right back," she promised in a gentle whisper.

He released her reluctantly, his fingers never quite loosening their hold as she slipped from his embrace. The lovely silk gown her sister had given her was at the foot of the bed. Karen undressed, almost wishing Rand could watch her as she removed each item of clothing and placed it aside.

Wordlessly, she went to him and slipped her arms around his neck, urging his mouth to hers. They were locked in a frantic embrace, an all-consuming desire. Trembling, she buried her face in his shirt, her body shuddering with the effort to breathe. Their kisses were now wild and fierce; his hands loosened her gown and leisurely caressed her.

Unbuttoning his shirt, she placed her hands on his hard ribs, gliding them upward over the hair of his chest, her fingers caressing and stroking as his heart thundered beneath her palm.

"Karen, Karen," he rasped, his mouth seizing hers in a passionate kiss. Deftly, his fingers released the tie of her gown and slipped it away. Her soft breasts seemed to sear his chest, and he groaned before kissing her lips, then descended lower, spreading a molten path of desire that left Karen quivering with anticipation. She clung to him, eager to give herself to his passion. It was a tender, intimate moment, and Rand hoarsely whispered his love as he parted her thighs and gently entered her trembling body. Karen's eyes widened at the sudden influx of pleasure; she arched against him, murmuring her love, and surrendered to the swirling excitement.

Afterward, they lay together, Rand's arms protectively holding her as she rested her head against the cushion of his chest. Each was spent by the fierceness of their lovemaking.

When they spoke, it was whispered phrases of love, their emotions too strong to express with mere words what their bodies had said for them. Soon they slept in a deep, untroubled slumber.

Karen woke around ten, the room dark and still. A surge of love for the man sleeping beside her overcame her, and she nestled closer in the haven of his arms. Rand loved her as she loved him; together, they would build a good life. With a languid sigh, she rested her head in the crook of his arm. Playfully, her fingers ran through the hair on his chest. When he stirred, she asked him softly, "Are you awake?"

Karen could hear the amusement in his voice. "How do you expect me to sleep with your fingers driving me insane?"

Karen laughed, her arms tightening around him. "I'm hungry."

Rand turned so his body lay above hers, his mouth parting her lips with an urgency that almost startled Karen.

"Rand." She pressed her face against his throat. "I'm hungry for food."

He paused, although his hands enjoyed the freedom of her pliant, soft body. A low protesting moan followed her words as she slid out of his arms and climbed from the bed.

"Do you want something?" she asked while tying the sash of her robe.

Rand raised his brows and sat upright. "Yes, but I think it'll have to wait."

With a smile of contentment, Karen wandered into the kitchen and fixed herself a sandwich. Her stomach growled, reminding her she hadn't eaten since breakfast.

Rand was on the phone when she entered the

bedroom. She sat on the bed, waiting for him to finish, her eyes studying the man she loved. There was a tenderness about him she hadn't seen before. The lines of fatigue were gone, and his eyes held a warm light.

"I've canceled my classes for tomorrow," he said, breaking into her thoughts. "It seems I have an urgent business matter that needs attending to at home." His eyes grew intense. "Come here, urgent matter."

A soft sigh slipped from her as she slid her arms around his neck. The thin piece of silk that was wrapped around her fell aimlessly to the floor.

"Karen," he groaned as his lips searched and found hers. She yielded to the urgency and clung to him, her smooth skin pressing against his muscular body. His touch was capable of drawing her strength as she responded to the intensity of his lovemaking. She was surprised by her abandonment as they came together again. They were caught in a whirlwind of spiraling sensations that hurled them upward to unscalable heights, then released them gently until they floated back to the reality of being in each other's arms.

They didn't speak; words would only diminish the wonder. Karen rested against him, and her cheek lay on his chest while he smoothed the tangles from her hair.

"I love you, Karen Prescott," he murmured softly; his voice contained a reverent note, as if he understood a love as deep as theirs could have been ordained only from above.

A loud ring roused Karen from the depths of sleep, but instead of reacting to the persistent peals, she incorporated them into her dream. Drawn naturally to the warmth beside her, she snuggled against Rand, folding her arms over his lean ribs. It was Rand's groggy "Hello" that brought her into reality.

Morning. Sunlight streamed into the window between a small crack in the drapery. With something akin to wonder, Karen marveled that she should be here with Rand, that they were man and wife, and that their love was secure and complete.

Unable to resist, she ran her fingers teasingly over his back. Rand shifted positions and sat upright. The telephone conversation continued, but it was distinctly a one-sided dialogue. All Rand murmured was "Yes," "good," "fine," "okay."

It must be Cora, Karen mused, and stiffened when Rand issued an invitation for dinner that evening. The woman wouldn't accept defeat easily, and an uncomfortable chill ran through Karen.

When Rand replaced the receiver, Karen slid her arms around his middle. "Good morning, Mr. Prescott," she whispered tenderly.

Rand turned, looping his arms around her, his face buried in the softness of her hair. "Good morning, Mrs. Prescott."

Tipping her head back, she gently stroked his chin and guided his mouth to hers to kiss him with a lingering warmth.

The hall clock chimed, reminding them it was well into morning.

"It would be easy to spend the whole day making love to my wife, but we're expecting company for dinner."

"Yes, I heard. What time is she coming?" A heavy sigh slipped from Karen. She didn't want this wonderful day to be ruined by Cora.

"She?" Rand's brow twisted dubiously.

"Wasn't that Cora on the phone?"

His mouth compressed into a taut line. "No, that was your father. He's coming to make sure his little girl is a happy bride. Believe me, the invitation for dinner was issued grudgingly."

"Dad?" Karen's thoughts raced furiously. "You mean that was my father on the phone?" she asked again in disbelief.

"Matthew McAlister, the blackmailer himself, is entering the lion's den."

Karen's face grew serious as she studied Rand sitting on the end of the bed. The initial rush of pleasure at waking with Rand at her side quickly faded. She went to him, holding his head against her abdomen, stroking the hair from his face. "I want us to talk to Dad tonight." Her voice was sober. "Perhaps then you will believe me. Your trust is important to me."

Gently, he pushed her away as if her nearness disturbed his resolve. When he stood, his back was facing her. The silence hung heavy between them until Rand spoke, his voice somber, quiet. "No, there's no need to discuss our situation with your father. He would naturally deny you had any part in the marriage trap. Trying to make me believe your innocence is all part of the game. I'm not a fool, nor am I stupid. You're my wife now, but I think it would be better if we never mentioned how we came into this marriage. Doing so would only bring bitterness between us. Is that understood, Karen?" He turned around, his face proud and strong.

She searched but could find no words to answer him.

"But, Rand, please…"

"Karen"—his tone was stern—"you do yourself more harm than good by insisting you're innocent. Now, I said I don't want to talk about it."

"All right," she murmured tightly. "We won't speak of it again."

Rand didn't want to argue; Karen could see it in his face as it relaxed, his look almost gentle. "Now, how about fixing me breakfast? I'm starved."

Karen swallowed the tightness lodged in her throat. "Starved?" she returned, forcing herself to shrug off the hurt. "My dear husband, you've been feasting all night." She tried to sound gay and lighthearted, but the word *husband* nearly stuck in her throat.

As their relationship stood now, she was little more than a glorified mistress. She yearned to satisfy far more than his physical desires; she wanted to share his joys, his burdens, the everyday rituals of life that make a wife a wife. Rand wouldn't accept that from her yet. Not until she'd proven herself, had earned his faith and trust. There was little he would accept from her other than the delights her body could give him. For now, she must be content with that. Did her father have any conception of the hellish situation he had cast her into? she wondered wearily.

"I *have* been feasting all night." Rand's words broke into her thoughts. "But I fear having you once is like drinking salt water. I'll never be satisfied." His arms slid around her waist, his mouth seeking the gentle curve of her neck. "But for right now," he murmured thickly, "I was referring to something more basic, like bacon and eggs."

Karen snuggled against him, resting her head on his shoulder. If Rand's desire for her was only physical, she would accept that. In time, she would be able to tear down the bitter walls he'd erected against her. Eventually, under the determined onslaught of her love, he would be her husband, and she would be his trusted, cherished wife.

"Bacon and eggs?" She sighed, feigning disappointment. "And I was prepared to satisfy another hearty appetite…" She wasn't allowed to finish the sentence.

With a laugh, Rand lifted her from the carpet and placed her on the bed, his fingers eagerly searching for the opening of her gown. The unexpected action took her breath away. Before she could object, his mouth greedily claimed hers. When his head lifted from hers, Karen gave a weak protest. "Rand, I was only teasing."

"Don't act so outraged, my love. You did offer to satisfy my appetites," he murmured before planting another hungry kiss on her open mouth.

Karen responded fully to his passion, moving her body against him provocatively...

It was a long time before either of them entered the kitchen.

They spent a portion of the day arranging Karen's things around the house so Rand knew their whereabouts. He had a complicated system regarding the placement of his clothes and personal items. It showed Karen again the difficulties he encountered with partial eyesight and reminded her never to leave her things lying around. In his home, it was difficult to remember that he had limited vision. His knowledge of the house and everything in it was complete. The old saying "a place for everything and everything in its place" certainly applied to the system Rand employed.

Karen was arranging her small collection of ballerina figures on the living-room bookcase when Rand spoke. "Karen," he said with a faint huskiness.

Her cheeks were flushed with a warm glow of satisfaction as she turned around. "Yes?"

"We forgot something last night."

"Impossible." She laughed lightly and circled her arms around his middle, tipping her head back to study his face. His smile was warm and sensuous; his eyes glowed with a happiness she knew came from her love. It was a heady realization that the love they shared could change so much in each of them.

Because of Rand, Karen saw life with clear, more revealing eyes. She found herself ready to listen to others the way Rand listened. She was willing to look beyond pretense with business associates and acquaintances.

With Rand, there had been a definite softening. He was more relaxed and not as apt to erect the angry facade he had worn when they first met. Even his iron-clad will had shown signs of a willingness to compromise.

"We forgot your wedding ring." Rand withdrew it from his pocket. It lay in the palm of his hand. The solitaire diamond slid to his fingertips, and he manipulated it as if his hands were familiar with its feel.

Karen glanced at her naked left hand. She didn't need a wedding band to say she was his wife. Ring or no ring, she would always belong to him.

"Karen." His voice was low and earnest. "I want more than a weekend marriage. I want you for a lifetime." He took her hand, his fingers caressing hers until he singled out the ring finger. With a tenderness that was almost reverent, he slid the ring on.

"I'll love you all my life, Karen Prescott," he whispered, as if it was a vow.

Instinctively, Karen's arms slid over his shoulders as she brought his mouth to hers. As their lips met, Karen felt him shudder as he buried his face in the dark curls that fell over her shoulder.

Later, they sauntered hand in hand over the grounds, talking and teasing. Following the trail, they strolled to the creek and back.

"Would you mind if I went back to work?" she quizzed, watching Rand's face. It was a question that had troubled Karen. Her own feelings were mixed; her mother had never worked outside the home, but Karen was sure she'd quickly find herself growing bored without the challenge of a job. Being a housewife would mean a drastic change in her lifestyle, and she wasn't sure she wanted to make the adjustment.

Rand shrugged. "That's entirely up to you. In my opinion, you were foolish to quit. Did you think I would demand your presence day and night?"

Karen stiffened defensively. "I quit because I was leaving Tacoma. I know you don't believe that, but it happens to be the truth."

His hand squeezed hers as if he wanted to punish her. "I thought we'd agreed to leave well enough alone? As for you returning to your job,

I really don't care. My hours are long, and I'm often not home until late. You might do well to have some outside interests."

Karen bit back the hurt, wishing she'd never asked Rand's opinion.

The sun was setting, leaving a red glow on the horizon, when Matthew arrived, bringing flowers and a bottle of wine. Karen answered the door hesitantly, unsure how she'd greet her father; her feelings were mixed and ambivalent. She was grateful Rand was still in the shower.

"'Tis a sad day when a father is forced to beg an invitation to his own daughter's," he announced gruffly, handing her his gifts.

"'Tis a sadder day when said daughter's honeymoon is interrupted," Karen chided in return.

He hugged her close, and when he spoke again, there was an odd ring in his voice.

"I've missed you, lass." He studied her intently for a long, sober minute.

Two days before, Karen would have ranted at her father, called him an interfering old fool. His impudence had cast her into a sea of misunderstandings, creating an almost insurmountable lack of trust between husband and wife. Instead, she gently kissed his weathered cheek. "I've missed you too, Dad."

Matthew watched his daughter closely. "Are you happy, lass?" he asked with concern. His eyes held a troubled light, as if he were seeking far more than his words implied. Approval? Forgiveness? Praise? Condemnation?

Matthew's face looked wan and drawn, as if he'd been under a great deal of stress, as he well might have been, wondering about Rand and Karen. Seeing the question in his eyes, she couldn't berate him. "I'm happy, Dad."

"Rand?" His eyes wavered from hers.

"In time," she offered gently.

Matthew grinned as if relieved of a burdensome load. "Didn't I tell you things had a way of working out for the best?" he said, chuckling.

"I think you should repeat that for Rand's benefit," she teased lovingly.

"Did I hear my name mentioned?" Rand entered the kitchen, his hair still wet from the shower, his smile welcoming.

Karen gave a grateful sigh. She wasn't sure how Rand would react to her father. That morning, he'd made it clear he didn't wish to confront Matthew with the details of the marriage, but Karen feared he might harbor some resentment against her father.

"Welcome to our home, Matthew," Rand greeted, and the two men shook hands, an unspoken understanding between them.

Matthew relaxed and started checking under

the lids of the pots bubbling on the stove top. "When's dinner?"

"Not until our other guest arrives," Karen said, trying to keep a straight face.

"Other guest?" Matthew quizzed.

Rand's brow wrinkled in question, but he didn't say anything.

"Yes, Dad. Rand invited the Widow Jackson."

Matthew's grin was wry until all three broke into hearty laughter.

While Karen placed the serving dishes on the table, she could hear Rand and her father laughing and joking together in the living room. She paused, watching them; her heart swelled with love for these two men. It was a relief beyond words that Rand showed no open hostility toward her father.

The lighthearted banter continued through dinner, and afterward, Rand challenged Matthew to a game of chess. Nothing could have pleased Karen's father more, and the board was soon set.

As before, Rand played the game entirely from memory. Karen moved the figures on his command, amazed how he could keep track of every move in his mind.

Matthew was an excellent player, and Rand a worthy opponent; the game dragged on, the skill of the two men evenly matched. Karen wasn't surprised when Rand won.

Matthew shook his head disbelievingly, moving the figures around the board, studying Rand's strategy.

Her eyes gleaming with pride, Karen turned and gave her husband a congratulatory hug.

"Well done, Prescott," Matthew said, but his eyes continued to study the board. "I accept defeat from you a second time, but want the chance to redeem myself."

With a lazy smile, Rand promised a rematch at a later date. Matthew left a short time later, and with a yawn, Karen closed and locked the front door behind him. Rand welcomed her into his arms with a smile.

"It's getting late," she whispered invitingly. Her fingers unbuttoned his shirt and teased his chest with light strokes before she wound her arms around his neck and drew his mouth down to hers.

Rand's lips moved hungrily over hers as he pressed her tightly against him until he shuddered with desire. "What is it about you?" he whispered thickly. "I'll never get enough of you, will I? Fifty years from now, I'll still be panting with desire for you." He led her purposefully toward their bedroom. Karen followed willingly but stopped at the doorway of one of the spare bedrooms, examining the room.

"This room will make a lovely nursery. What do you think, Rand?"

He stopped and became suddenly very still, his mouth drawn in a taut line. "I think there's something you'd better understand right now. There will be no children as a result of our marriage."

A shocked silence followed his announcement. Karen stared at him disbelievingly. "No children? But why?"

"For heaven's sake, Karen, think about it," he said bitterly. "I'm in no position to be any kind of father. Nor do I want children; they're an encumbrance I can live without."

"You're being unfair."

"Unfair?" He gave a short, derisive laugh. "You're a fine one to talk. If it had been up to me, I wouldn't have had a wife, either. If you want to talk about unfair, then we can talk about you and your father."

The cruel words struck her harder than any blow. "But, Rand…" she pleaded, then halted. A brooding scowl darkened his face, and Karen knew him well enough to recognize that arguing was useless.

"You got what you wanted, Karen. We're married, but from here on, I make the decisions, and there will be no children. I don't ever want to discuss the subject again. The matter is closed." His tone was emphatic and hard as he strode away angrily, leaving her standing speechless in the hall.

An ache began to grow within her heart. She was married to Rand, a dream she believed would fulfill her every desire. But the deep womanly need to bear his child would be denied her. How easy it was to picture a dark-haired baby boy; Karen shook her head to cast the picture from her mind. Silently, she walked into their bedroom.

Rand was sitting at the end of their bed, bent forward, his face in his hands. He straightened when he heard her enter. "Karen, listen, it's bad enough having a wife I'll never see. I won't endure the same agony with a child." A hand moved wearily across his face. "Trust me in this. I know what you're feeling, but give us a chance. Together we'll build a good life; we don't need anything else."

Pictures of James and Carter flashed through her mind; she knew the love she felt for her two nephews was only a fraction of the emotion she would experience for her own child. She looked away; the searing, raw disappointment left an aching void in her heart. Gently, she went to him and traced the determined line of his jaw.

"Shall I take the precautions, or will you?" she asked in a tortured whisper.

Nine

"Karen?"

Faintly, she could hear Rand's call and carefully rolled from the bed. But when she attempted to straighten, her muscles knotted in protest.

"I'm coming," she called, stopping to rub the small of her back. When she limped down the hall from their bedroom, she could hear Carl's worried voice.

"All day she was out there. Wouldn't let me help; said I had enough to do without adding a garden to the list. Your missus is going to be real sore, mark my words. Real sore."

"Hi, honey. How was your day?" She greeted Rand cheerfully, belying the discomfort of her aching muscles. Her eyes narrowed as they fell on Carl. She could tell Rand of her foolishness herself; Carl didn't need to do it for her.

"I'm fine," Rand answered shortly. "What's

this Carl is telling me about you working out-side all day?"

"It wasn't all day," she denied, and winced from a shooting pain in her back. "It seems certain people are cursed with loose tongues around here. Isn't that right, Carl?"

The older man shuffled his feet, avoiding her eyes. "I'll be going home now." He turned to leave, but not before Karen saw the smile that crinkled the crow's-feet about his eyes.

Karen moved closer to Rand, wrapping her arms around his waist, then groaned softly. "Kiss me if you must, but please be gentle."

Rand scowled. "You crazy little fool. What were you doing, shoveling hard dirt?" He was both bemused and angry. He released her, and instantly Karen missed the warmth of his touch.

"I thought I'd plant a garden," she explained, flexing her overworked muscles, then flinch-ing because even the slightest movement hurt. "My mother had a big garden every year. I don't think I ever realized how much work she put into it. The most I did was pull weeds. Believe me, I appreciate her efforts more fully now."

"If you wanted a garden, why didn't you say something?" he questioned, the irritation leav-ing his face. "I could have had someone come and rototill for you." He brought her back into the circle of his arms, his fingers gently rubbing the back of her neck.

His touch did insane things to her equilibrium, and she swayed against him. "I don't know," she responded huskily, her eyes closed, savoring the gentle caress of his hands. "I forgot, I guess." Clear thinking was almost impossible when Rand was holding her like this. His hands molded over her buttocks, lifting her pliant body against him. "Don't stop," she pleaded.

Rand's voice was low and husky as he murmured against her skin. "I have no intention of stopping."

Karen gave a sighing laugh. "I was referring to the massage. I could use a good rubdown."

With soft kisses, Rand closed her eyes. Again, the pressure of his arms increased as he lifted and carried her into the bedroom.

His fingers were soothing and gentle as he manipulated the sore muscles. Her flesh responded to the overwhelming comfort of his touch. She was encompassed in warmth; a fury of sensation assaulted her, and she yearned to roll over and bring his mouth to hers. Anything to satisfy this aching void he was creating within her. A small cry of pleasure slipped from her parted lips. But if Rand knew what he was doing to her, he ignored her plea until she released another soft moan.

His hand settled over her shoulder to gently turn her. Karen stared for a moment at the intensity that burned from his eyes. "You know what I want," he murmured thickly before lowering his mouth to hers.

A long time later, they rested, Karen's head nestled in the crook of Rand's arm. His fingers continued to explore her body by leisurely tracing an imaginary line around her breasts. The rounded flesh seemed to swell at his caress.

The meandering pattern followed down her abdomen. "I believe you're gaining weight."

"I know." She smiled, leisurely reveling in the power of his touch to arouse her. "It's Dorothy's recipes, but if you notice it, too, then it's time to go on a diet."

"Just as long as you only abstain from food," he whispered, claiming her mouth in a searing kiss that left her breathless.

Rand's breathing wasn't any more even, and when he spoke, there was a hoarse quality to his voice. "I have some news."

"Good or bad?"

A smile lifted the corners of his full mouth. "I'll let you decide. I've been asked to participate in a lecture series across the country. The schedule isn't completed yet, but I imagine I'll be gone two, possibly three weeks."

The smile died on Karen's face, and she

closed her eyes to block the loneliness a long separation would bring. Tears burned for release, and she brushed them away, angry with herself for being so emotional. "Will Cora be with you?" she questioned after a while.

"Of course Cora will be with me." His voice held a mocking note. "We are partners, you know."

"I thought we were partners, too? Remember me? I'm the wife you promised to love and cherish. I don't exactly relish twiddling my thumbs for several weeks while you go gallivanting across the country with another woman."

A scowl darkened Rand's face. "Karen, this isn't like you. Cora isn't another woman in the sense you're implying."

"Not from lack of trying, I bet," she snapped childishly, pulling herself from his arms and sitting upright.

"Karen?" Rand's voice held a puzzled note. His hands slipped over her shoulders to bring her back. "As for us being partners, if you recall…"

Abruptly, Karen twisted away. "Are you going to throw the fact you didn't want to marry me in my face every time we have an argument? You don't need to tell me your feelings on the matter. Believe me, actions speak louder than words."

"Karen, would you kindly listen to me?" he demanded, his mouth thinning angrily.

With her back facing him, she responded stiffly, "I'm listening."

"You could have fooled me," Rand murmured under his breath. Then he began again slowly. "Now, what I've been trying to say is this: Cora and I have been invited to participate in a lecture series. We have accepted the invitation. But there is no reason why you should stay here without me. I want you to accompany me on this trip."

"Oh." The anger drained from her all in one breath. "Oh," she said again, feeling chagrined and stupid. What was the matter with her? Why was she acting like such a shrew? "In that case, I'd like to do two things," she said softly, swallowing her pride. "First, I want to apologize for being so hotheaded, and second, I want you to know how very pleased I'd be to travel with you."

"Good," Rand said simply, holding her again.

Suddenly Karen came to the realization that Rand was trusting her now as he'd never done before.

Karen woke the next morning stiff and more than a little sore. When she started to get out of bed, she moaned as her stomach heaved unsteadily. Lying back against the pillow, she took deep breaths, afraid she would be sick.

"Rand," she murmured tightly, "I think I really must have done too much yesterday. I feel awful."

Tenderly, he brushed the hair from her face and kissed her forehead. "Stay in bed. I'll phone later and see how you're feeling."

"I'll be fine. Don't worry about me. Oh, if I'm not here, don't worry. Judy and I are taking the boys to Point Defiance Zoo. I'd hate to disappoint them."

"They can make the trip without you," Rand said, tucking in his shirt. His brow was knit with concern.

"I won't go unless I feel better," she promised.

Rand's kiss was gentle as he tucked the blankets over her shoulders.

Karen watched him go, her heart full of love. After several weeks of married life, she was beginning to discover the joys and benefits of being Rand's wife. As he claimed, his hours were often long as he worked with Cora on a textbook they were compiling. Karen often waited up for him on the sofa, sometimes falling asleep. She'd been so tired lately. Rand woke her, rousing her by spreading tender kisses over her face. Drowsily, Karen would loop her arms around his neck and direct him to her moist lips.

The evenings he was home, Karen would read aloud while they sat together, Rand's arms securely wrapped around her. Their taste in literature was surprisingly similar, and they explored everything from Kipling to Tolkien. In bed, she desired him as much as he desired her. Rand was the perfect lover, patient, tender, coaxing. They never spoke of the reasons for their marriage, but it was almost as if their love and need for each other had brought them together.

After a two-hour tour of the zoo and park, they were all hungry and tired. Dark clouds began rolling in to threaten the picnic that had been planned and packed so carefully.

"I wanna stay," Carter objected, ignoring the first drops of rain.

"We aren't going to let a little rain stop us, are we?" James echoed his dissatisfaction.

A few intermittent drops quickly became a fierce downpour, and the four ran to the parking lot without further discussion.

"I still want to have a picnic." Carter's voice dripped with disappointment as he climbed into the backseat of the car.

"Let's wait a few minutes; maybe it'll stop," Karen offered encouragingly. "If not, we'll have a special picnic at my house."

"All right!" both boys chimed.

"If we're going to wait here, I'll pour us some coffee." Judy opened the top of the thermos, and Karen's stomach pitched at the aroma.

She shook her head dismissively. "None for me, thanks. I don't know what it is, but coffee doesn't agree with my stomach lately."

Judy jerked her head up, and the liquid sloshed over the side of the cup and onto the seat. "Karen," she whispered in disbelief, eyeing her sister intently, "the first few months I was pregnant with James, I couldn't tolerate the taste or smell of coffee. I knew almost immediately when I was going to have Carter because the same thing happened. Even before the doctor confirmed my condition."

Karen gave a low laugh. "Well, I'm not pregnant. In fact, I'm sure I'm not," she said, more to assure herself than Judy. "Oh, heavens! Rand would be furious."

"What's pregnant?" Carter questioned, leaning over from the backseat.

"I'll explain later," Judy promised, studying Karen's worried expression.

A half hour later, the four were positioned under Karen's dining-room table, eating their lunch, when Rand entered through the front door.

"Karen, I'm home," he announced, shaking the rain off his umbrella.

Normally, Karen was there to greet Rand, but James and Carter were intent on playing a game of hide-and-seek.

"I'm here," squeaked James in an attempt to imitate Karen.

"James? Carter? Okay, boys, what tricks are you up to now? I suppose you've got your aunt tied up outside somewhere." He arched an amused brow toward the sound of their voices.

"Rand's certainly got my boys pegged," Judy whispered.

"We're under the table." Karen laughed as she watched his dark-trousered leg walk toward her.

"Under the what?"

"Come and join us; we're having a picnic," Judy explained, stifling her own laughter.

"It's times like these that make me wonder just exactly what kind of a family I married into." His face was smiling as he knelt down. "Just what will be required of me before I can talk to my wife?" he quizzed suspiciously.

"I'm here, Rand." Karen edged her way between bodies, sandwiches, and Number Nine to meet her husband. "Sit down and make yourself at home," she invited, and placed a welcoming kiss on his puzzled brow.

"May I remind you, I am home!" Humor glinted briefly in his expression. "I'm almost afraid to ask this, but just why are you eating your lunch under the table?"

"Because it's raining," the boys explained simultaneously.

"True," he reasoned, "but not inside the house."

"Well, it wouldn't be a picnic on top of the table, would it?" Karen asked him with an impatient sigh.

"There's logic in this someplace, but I swear it's beyond me." The humor in his smile held a wealth of love and warmth.

Karen regarded him curiously. "You're home awfully early. Is anything wrong?"

"Can't a husband come home early? May I remind you we've only been married a short while." His husky voice held a suggestive note, and Karen flushed.

"Finish your lunch, boys." Judy tipped her head back and winked knowingly at her sister. "It's time we left."

"There's no need to rush," Karen said, but she didn't insist they stay. Rand was rarely home early, and she selfishly wanted him to herself.

The picnic items were quickly packed while the boys protested. Judy ushered them out the door, and it suddenly became very quiet without the chatter of the two boys.

"Would you like some lunch? Are you hungry?" Rand stood beside her, and she turned, sliding her arms around his middle. Tilting her head back, she watched his expression alter.

"Starving." His mouth explored the side of her neck and sent shivers of delight shooting down her body.

"What would you like?" She melted against him, her heart thundering wildly.

"Don't ask silly questions," he whispered before claiming her mouth in a flaming kiss that left her weak and clinging. When he led her into their bedroom, Karen had no intention of protesting.

The nagging suspicion Karen was pregnant became a reality as the days passed. She'd refused to acknowledge the early signs, but there could be no denying the slight thickening of her waist or the added fullness of her breasts. Now it wasn't only coffee that upset her stomach; the smell of certain foods, especially bacon, would cause her to wretch. She found herself irritable, and it didn't seem to matter how much sleep she got, for she was constantly tired.

The first morning she lost her breakfast was the day Karen accepted the truth. Deathly pale and still nauseated, she staggered back to the bedroom and lay down.

With her arms cradling her stomach, she

closed her eyes and let out a low moan of despair. "No, please, God, no." Rand would never believe she hadn't purposely gotten pregnant. The knowledge was sure to destroy the budding trust between them. She had worked so hard to gain his confidence in her integrity. How would she ever tell him? No possible explanation would make things right. And his reaction would defy comprehension.

Forcing herself to dress, she brushed her teeth, still feeling wretched and miserable. Her reflection in the bathroom mirror told her she looked as rotten as she felt.

Her sister had advised her to make an appointment with the doctor as soon as possible. But Karen had delayed, hoping against Las Vegas odds that she had some weird, unexplainable virus. *Some virus,* she mused. Her fingers trembled when she made the call. She wouldn't say anything to Rand until she was sure. His mother was coming for a visit, and she couldn't tell him before then.

Depression as heavy as Karen had ever experienced weighed on her. A baby. She found her hands resting on her abdomen while a myriad of emotions filled her all at once. A gentle smile touched her lips. A baby. This should be one of the most glorious days of her life, knowing that the love they shared had created this life growing within her.

Love. What a strange emotion, but not really an emotion at all; more an act of the will. Certainly it wasn't anything she could define. Did Rand really love her? Could she be totally secure in his love? He desired her physically. Was that love? He had accused and doubted her regarding their marriage. Was that love? As sure as the sun would rise on the morrow, he would doubt her again when he learned of this pregnancy. Was that love?

Hiding her symptoms from Rand became a worrisome game. The mornings she was especially ill, she would complain of being overly tired and stay in bed. Rand would lovingly accuse her of being lazy. Karen watched him dress, praying he'd hurry while she took deep breaths to delay the inevitable. The minute he was out the door, Karen would rush to the bathroom to empty her stomach.

Judy recommended eating soda crackers before rising in the morning to relieve the nausea. But when Rand complained of crumbs between the sheets and accused her of cheating on her diet, Karen laughed and promised not to eat in bed again.

A hundred times, she was grateful Rand couldn't see her. One look at her pale, bloodless cheeks and he would have guessed her condition immediately. That he hadn't put the facts together knotted Karen's stomach with guilt. His trust in her had become so complete that he didn't even suspect.

Karen was sure Carl knew. More than once she found his eyes following her, his look concerned and worried. She wasn't sure if he was anxious because she was obviously having such a bad time with the morning sickness or if he realized what this child would do to her and Rand's relationship. Either way, her eyes silently pleaded with him not to say anything. The look he returned assured her that he would not betray a confidence.

There was another problem Karen had yet to resolve. Number Nine was obviously pregnant.

"But Carl," Karen had protested, "I thought you said you'd taken her to the vet and everything had been taken care of."

"All her shots." Carl looked away nervously. "Number Nine was just a kitten then, and the vet wanted to wait a few weeks before having her spayed. I assumed you realized that. I'm sorry, Miss Karen."

She sighed in defeat. She couldn't be angry with Carl; it hadn't been his fault. If she hadn't been so wrapped up in her own problems, she would have known something was wrong when all the male cats started prowling around.

"Don't worry, Carl," she reassured him with a weak smile. "I'm sure Rand will understand."

"I'm sure he will, too," Carl told her, and Karen had the funny feeling he wasn't referring to the cat.

"But I don't understand how it could have happened." Karen's eyes pleaded with the doctor.

"It's not unusual for a pregnancy to occur even with the appropriate precautions, but judging from the look of things, I'd say you were already pregnant when you came for your first visit." Dr. Marshall offered Karen a reassuring smile. Since she was obviously so upset with her condition, he took the time to talk with her and answer her questions in a gentle, reassuring manner.

"Already pregnant?" Karen stared back in disbelief.

"I'm afraid so. I'd guess you were close to three months pregnant."

"Three months?" she whispered incredulously. Had she been so obtuse that she had not recognized even the most obvious signs? Dazed and unsure, Karen responded to the remainder of the appointment with little more than feeble nods.

Judy was waiting for her in the reception area. "Well?" She rose expectantly as Karen entered the larger room.

Karen stared at her sister with sightless eyes. "The doctor thinks I may be as much as three months along—"

"Karen." Although she shared her sister's anxiety, Judy didn't bother to disguise her pleasure. "Good grief, you won't be hiding this from Rand much longer. When do you plan on telling him?"

"I don't think it's a matter of when but how I'm going to tell him," Karen answered.

"But, Karen, the longer you delay, the more likely he is to guess."

"I know." Karen expelled her breath and looked to her sister helplessly. "I'll tell him soon."

After his mother's visit, Karen promised herself. Judy's look was skeptical.

Each day, Karen answered her sister's inquiring gaze with a negative shake of her head.

Rand had described his mother perfectly, and when she stepped off the plane, Karen spotted her instantly.

Eileen Prescott was tall and slender. Her blue business suit, smart and stylish, was a pleasant contrast to her hair, which was completely gray, cut fashionably short. There wasn't a striking resemblance between mother and son, but it wasn't difficult to tell the two were related.

"I see her," Karen said nervously.

"Relax, Karen. My mother's going to love you." His hand, resting on her shoulder, gave her an encouraging squeeze.

With swift, bold strides, Eileen Prescott walked directly to Rand. Karen stepped aside as mother embraced son.

She gave him a surly look. "Well, introduce me. I didn't fly two thousand miles to look at your dour face."

There was an affectionate smile in Rand's eyes as he held his arms open for Karen's return. "Mother, this is my wife, Karen."

Karen moved forward, still in awe of this overpowering woman. "Welcome to Tacoma, Mrs. Prescott." Her senses were clamoring under the woman's cold, unfriendly gaze.

Eileen ignored Karen's welcome. "Why, Rand, she's barely more than a teenager." It was the same gruff tone as before.

Karen eased herself closer to Rand, embarrassed and uncomfortable. The welcoming smile died on Rand's face, and he spoke sharply. "Woman enough, Mother."

Eileen ignored his tone and returned her attention to Karen. "I understand your father was an immigrant. The Prescotts can trace their family tree back to the sixteen hundreds. I expected Rand to marry within his own class," she stated stiffly, as if she doubted Karen's legitimacy.

The assertion stung. The McAlisters were of proud Scottish descent, and what they lacked in heritage was compensated for in pride. Karen bit back angry words, but Rand felt no such restraint and snapped angrily.

"Are you sure you wouldn't like to check out her teeth?"

There was dead silence. Eileen's severe expression altered to a twinkling smile, and she laughed, smiling at Karen with satisfaction. "Welcome to the family, Karen, such as it is." She stepped forward and gave her daughter-in-law a vivacious squeeze.

Astonished at the extreme change in mood, Karen was at a loss for words but managed a tremulous smile. "Thank you."

In the days that followed, Karen came to respect her unpretentious mother-in-law. Her manner was sometimes surly and forward, but it didn't take long for Karen to discover her warm and sincere heart.

Eileen discovered Karen's secret the first morning of her visit. As soon as Rand was out the door to school, Karen slumped in the chair, feeling wretched.

Eileen was waiting for her with a damp wash-cloth. "Are you going to be sick?" she asked abruptly.

Karen shook her head, closing her eyes to ward off the nausea. She was used to the gruff tone of her voice. Eileen spoke with a brusque affection that couldn't offend.

"I'm fine." Karen looked away.

Her mother-in-law's smile was tender and knowing. "Does Rand know?"

Miserably, she gave a negative shake. "Rand has made it very clear he doesn't want children. I don't know how I'm going to tell him."

"Doesn't seem to me he has much choice in the matter. He's going to be a father, like it or not." She made it sound so simple and matter-of-fact.

"I wish it were that easy."

"He can't place the blame entirely on you... it does take two. That son of mine can be such a fool sometimes. Leave him to me. I'll set him straight."

"No, don't. It's important that I be the one to tell him," Karen pleaded, and sat down as another wave of nausea threatened.

"Well, you'll have to tell him soon. I've been here less than a day and guessed almost immediately. Don't be a ninny about it. He's bound to be unhappy for a while, but he loves you." She paused and chuckled. "Rand surprised the heck out of me at the airport the way he stepped in to protect you. I didn't know he had it in him. First time he's raised his voice to me in twenty years." She laughed again, as if finding the whole situation amusing.

"He's my husband; it was only natural—" Karen began.

"Not so," Eileen interrupted quickly. "Rand and I have a special mother-son relationship. His father died when Rand was eleven. George was working in Alaska; we were desperately in need of extra money for Rand's medical expenses. We traveled from doctor to doctor, seeking the latest professional skill for his deteriorating eyesight, but no one could offer us hope. The public schools weren't equipped to teach the boy, and it meant sending him to expensive boarding schools for the blind. All this took money, so George accepted this high-risk, high-paying job in Alaska. He was there two years before being killed in a mining accident. The only frivolous thing he ever sent home was that locket you're wearing. It arrived after we received word George had been killed. I never could wear the thing; too many sad memories."

Karen fingered the locket that hung around

her neck. It did hold special significance to Rand, perhaps because he assumed their love would end with the same bittersweet memories.

"Rand seemed to blame himself for George's death. Nothing I could say would lessen his guilt." Eileen continued speaking; even after all this time, reliving the memory proved painful. "In all the years since, Rand has been a model son. He's cared for my every need, given me every consideration. When he stood up to me the way he did at the airport, I knew he loved you. I needed to be assured of that. Things were mighty fishy when he arrived for his so-called honeymoon with that other woman. I've been wanting him to marry for years. He needs a wife, and selfishly, I wouldn't be opposed to a few grandchildren, but Rand would laugh and quickly change the subject. He mentioned you first thing off the plane, but I wondered what he was doing bringing me Cora when I wanted to meet you."

"Eileen?" Karen's fingers clenched tightly together in a nervous action.

"Speak up; I can't be expected to hear you if you insist on talking to the floor."

"Rand...Rand didn't exactly want to marry me." Karen flushed as she related the events leading up to their wedding.

"Lordy me, your daddy's one sly devil." She

laughed brusquely. "I can well imagine Rand's reaction to that," she said, laughing all the more.

Karen looked away.

"Don't look so put out. Rand wasn't totally opposed to this marriage, or nothing on God's good earth would have persuaded him to marry you. Being pressured was sure to ruffle a few of his proud feathers, but I know my son well enough to tell you he would have rotted in hell rather than marry someone he didn't want."

"But don't you see?" Karen murmured dismally. "He's sure to believe I tricked him with this pregnancy."

"No doubt he'll be as angry as a wounded bear, but given time, he'll come around. Now, don't be a quitter; give him time to sort through his feelings. If he said he was opposed to a family, it's not because he doesn't like children. Rand will make an excellent father. My only advice to you is to tell him soon. It's bound to go better for you if he hears it from your lips than if he discovers it on his own."

Acknowledging the wisdom of her mother-in-law, Karen had to agree.

Eileen returned to New York four days later, leaving with Karen's promise that she'd tell Rand about the baby soon.

Karen mentally prepared herself all the next

day, determined to tell Rand about the baby right after dinner.

"It was nice having my mother for a visit, but quite frankly, I'm glad she's gone. I like having you to myself." Rand sat on the sofa, pulling Karen onto his lap; his fingers wasted no time unbuttoning her blouse.

Abruptly, Karen twisted away and stood. "Rand, no, don't touch me, please."

"Karen?" He sounded surprised by her sudden rejection.

She stood across the room from him, rigid with apprehension. Her hand rested protectively on the slight swelling of her stomach. "Rand," she told him boldly, her voice tight, "I'm going to have a baby."

Ten

The room crackled with a stunned silence; Rand expelled an uneven, disbelieving breath before his jaw tightened ominously. Despair flickered over his face, and he paused to run his fingers through his hair wearily. He was silent for so long, Karen didn't know how much more tension she could endure.

"Yell, scream, do what you need to do. But please, don't just sit there." She felt far more capable of dealing with his anger than the tormented ache in his eyes.

"All my life I've had to deal with people who feel that because I'm handicapped, I must also be mentally retarded. I expected more from you, Karen."

His words stabbed at her heart. She yearned to go to him, hold him, reassure him, anything but this intolerable, tortured look. He resembled a man defeated and friendless. He slouched forward, burying his face in his hands.

"I realize this is of little comfort to either of us at the moment, but I want you to know the doctor says I was already pregnant when I went to see him about birth control." Her voice faltered slightly.

Rand's head snapped up, his eyes blazing. The short, abrupt laugh was full of malice. "Get out."

Karen stared at him with disbelieving eyes.

"I said get out," he raged in white fury.

She choked back a sob, her voice raw as she spoke. "Just how far do you want me to go? Out of the room? Out of the house? Out of your life?"

Violently, Rand swung around, his hand slamming against the lamp, sending it crashing into the coffee table. The ceramic base shattered into a thousand pieces as his anger exploded.

Karen backed away from him fearfully as he stumbled from the living room. The picture windows vibrated as he slammed the front door.

Where would he go? Karen looked around her with the most helpless feeling in the world. A knot in her throat was so tight she could barely swallow. Her first inclination was to run after him, plead with him to understand. But it was useless, and she knew it. Miserably, she picked up the larger pieces of the broken lamp.

There was no use attempting to sleep; she couldn't until Rand was home. The car was gone; apparently, he had gotten Carl to drive him someplace. Possibly Cora's? She quickly cast the pain-inducing thought from her mind. A long time later, she heard the soft purr of the car engine as it died, and she sighed with relief. But Rand didn't come into the house. The time grew so long that Karen nervously stared out the window, hoping to see him. The yard—everywhere she could see—was deserted. Why did she have to love him so much? Why couldn't she just go to bed and let him work out the problem his own way? She'd been shocked, too, when she'd first realized she wasn't suffering from some obscure virus.

Was he walking in the woods? It was dark; he could hurt himself. Another half hour passed, each second interminable. Karen couldn't stand it anymore and carelessly threw a sweater over her shoulders.

"Rand?" she called, venturing down the path leading to the woods. "Please answer me."

The night was so clear and still. She stopped to listen, but everything was deadly quiet until Karen wanted to cry with frustration.

"Miss Karen," Carl spoke from behind her, and Karen swiveled around.

"Where's Rand?" Her eyes pleaded with him.

"I don't know." The older man's eyes avoided hers. "He had me take him to a bar, said he didn't want me to wait. But he was in a bad way; real angry, he was. I sat outside for a long time, wondering what to do. When I went back inside, Mr. Rand was gone."

Karen's hand squeezed Carl's arm. "I told Rand about the baby."

Carl's smile was wry. "I figured as much. Give him time; he'll come around. It won't be long before he'll be handing me a cigar as proud as any father; you wait and see."

Tears shimmered in Karen's eyes, tears of hope. "Thank you. I needed to hear that."

Carl patted her shoulder gently. "Do you want me to wait up with you? Neither of us is going to sleep until he's home."

"Dorothy?" Karen's gaze flickered back to Carl's house.

"Been asleep for hours." He chuckled softly.

With a slight nod, Karen accepted the man's kind offer. They walked to the house together.

Several hours later, the sound of a door closing and someone singing told them Rand was home. The words of the song were slurred and barely discernible.

"WHATCHA GONNA DO WITH A DRUNKEN BLIND MAN? WHATCHA GONNA DO WITH A DRUNKEN BLIND MAN? EARL-LIE IN THE MORNING."

Carl was immediately at Rand's side while Karen paid the taxi driver. The man gave her a sympathetic smile and drove into the night.

Rand's weight was giving Carl trouble as they weaved toward the bedroom. Karen hurried to help, slipping her arm around Rand's waist, accepting a portion of his weight as his arm fell haphazardly across her shoulders.

Rand staggered slightly, then paused as if suddenly realizing Karen was there.

"Karen, my sweet Karen." A haunted, tortured look came over his masculine features. His mouth twisted into a dark, foreboding glower. Angrily, he pushed her aside.

"Trick the blind man. Hurt the blind man. Fool the blind man," he shouted, madly waving his arms.

No one was more surprised than Karen when Carl unexpectedly lifted Rand, placing his bulk over his shoulder like a fireman. When Carl laid him on the bed, Rand was either asleep or dead drunk.

"He'll be all right until morning," Carl assured Karen as he stopped to remove Rand's shoes.

Numbly, Karen took a blanket from the hall

closet, and laid it over his still body. A few minutes later, she walked Carl to the door. When she returned to the bedroom, Rand was making sleeping noises, lost to the world. Gently, she touched his face, the weight of unhappiness bearing hard upon her shoulders.

She slept in the spare bedroom, the room she thought would make a lovely nursery. It seemed fitting somehow. When she woke, Rand had already left for school. She looked at the unkempt bed and experienced a bittersweet agony. Trailing her fingers across the pillow that had held his head, she was hoping to draw some solace. Instead, she experienced an acute loneliness.

Rand wasn't home for dinner. Carl phoned to say Rand was working late with Cora, but she guessed the call had been made on his own initiative. It was after midnight before she went to bed, lying awake until she heard Rand enter. He undressed in the dark, pulled back the covers on his side, and climbed into bed. Their bodies were only a few inches apart, yet a whole world lay between them. Karen was completely still, willing Rand to say something, anything. After a while, she abandoned the hope and with an agonizing sigh drifted into sleep.

First thing the next morning, she woke again, experiencing the now-familiar waves of nausea. Deep breaths didn't help, and she rushed into the bathroom. When she straightened, she found Rand's large frame blocking the doorway.

"Are you all right?" he questioned tightly.

"I'm fine." Rand looked as drawn and pale as she did.

"Does this happen often?" he asked again, gruffly.

Karen's voice sounded choked and small. "Sometimes two or three times a week."

His face twisted into a vicious smile, almost as if he was pleased she was experiencing some discomfort with this pregnancy. "Next time, close the bathroom door. The sound of you vomiting isn't a pleasant way to wake up."

"All right," Karen agreed, hoping to hide the hurt in her voice.

Leaving early and coming home later and later was a pattern Rand followed rigidly the next few days. Karen rarely saw him, and if she did, he didn't speak to her unless it was in gruff, impatient tones.

He was obviously overworking himself, skipping meals and not getting enough sleep. Karen's tortured gaze followed him.

Rand had told her to get out, but seemed unwilling to tell her how far he wanted her to go. The temptation was strong to pack her things, but Karen had never been a quitter, and this marriage was worth saving. If anything, her resolve to work things out grew stronger as the days passed.

Saturday morning, Karen woke with a queasy stomach but held her own until after breakfast; then she was sick again.

"Isn't there anything you can do about this?" Rand asked her impatiently after she reappeared in the kitchen.

"I'm usually okay if I can force down some soda crackers first thing. I try to keep some on the nightstand…" She paused at the look of disgust that came over Rand's face.

His upper lip curled into a snarl. "Those were the crumbs I felt in bed, weren't they?"

"Yes." She wouldn't lie to him even if it meant condemning herself.

Karen had never seen anyone's look turn as cold or hard.

"You're a deceitful bitch, Karen."

"Can't you understand?" she snapped. "I didn't plan this pregnancy."

"Just like you didn't plan our marriage?"

Karen dropped her eyes, her hands clenched tightly at her sides. It was no use trying to reason with Rand, nor would she again. If he loved her, truly loved her, then his faith in her integrity would eventually overcome his doubts. She couldn't force the issue.

Perhaps his irritation wouldn't have been so explosive if he hadn't gone to stroke the cat and discovered she was pregnant.

"Karen." His voice had vibrated through the house. When she didn't respond immediately, he shouted again.

She'd gone to the bedroom, taking her time. She wouldn't rush to him; she wasn't a servant who responded to threats and yelling. "What is it?" she asked calmly, ignoring his scowl.

"The cat." Anger furrowed his brow, and his mouth curved in a taut line. "Number Nine is pregnant, isn't she?" It wasn't a question, but an accusation, as if this, too, were something Karen had purposely done to thwart and undermine his authority.

"Yes," she responded simply, without explanation.

"Why wasn't I warned of the blessed event?" he demanded sarcastically.

She replied in mocking tones, "I would have been more than pleased to tell you, but I haven't seen you in nearly a week. And, shall we say, the timing was wrong."

Karen had never seen anyone angrier. His hands were knotted into tight fists; his dark eyes became as hard as steel, his jawline white and tense. "Get rid of the cat." The softly spoken words were more menacing than if he'd raged at her.

Karen gasped in disbelief; all attempts at impudence collapsed with his words. "You don't mean that."

His lip curled sardonically as he moved past her and into the den, his message clear.

Later, Karen went for a walk. Tears stung her eyes, and she tilted her head back to prevent their spilling. She followed the worn path leading into the woods and heard Carl's approach before she saw him. Hurriedly, she wiped the tears from her eyes and put on a bright smile.

"Good morning, Miss Karen." He greeted her with a broad grin.

"Been leaving little tidbits around for the animals again, I see." She responded in a teasing banter, belying the hurt that lay just below the surface of her smile.

He chuckled, and the sound of his amusement lifted her soul from the mire of self-pity. Likable, lovable, understanding Carl. Why did life have to be so complicated? Why couldn't she be more like this man, who wore a ready smile and looked as if he'd never known trouble or discouragement?

"Carl?"

"Yes'm."

"Rand found out about Number Nine."

The older man chuckled again. "I've been wondering about that bellow that came from your house this morning. Was he angry?"

Karen couldn't prevent a smiling response to his humor. Rand had sounded like a bull elk in his irritation. "He wasn't exactly pleased. I have to find another home for Number Nine."

The smile faded from Carl's weathered face. "I don't think he means that, Miss Karen. He seems to be saying a lot of things he doesn't mean lately." The dark eyes grew intense. "Me and the missus will take Number Nine. If Mr. Rand doesn't want her back, that's fine, 'cause we've been needing a mouser."

"But she's going to deliver the litter soon."

"Not to worry." Again, Karen was reassured with a grin. "We have several friends who need mousers."

Karen was afraid that if she spoke, her voice would crack and Carl would know how much his generosity had affected her.

Eyes dancing, he touched the tip of his cap and sauntered down the path.

"Carl?" she called after he'd gone several feet.

He spun around.

"Thank you." She couldn't hide the choke in her voice.

As she continued walking along the well-worn path, she could think, sort through her own feelings. For all the unhappiness she was experiencing, there was also a budding excitement beginning to blossom. A child was growing within her, a child created in love.

Rand and Karen were scheduled to leave for the lecture series next week. The thought of time alone together brought a surge of hope. Rand had purposely made separate flight plans so they wouldn't be traveling with Cora. He'd promised to make this trip the honeymoon they'd never had. Karen believed that only when they were separated from the pressures around them would Rand begin to accept the child. Six days; she could last another six days. The lecture series offered hope and promise.

When she returned to the house feeling refreshed and invigorated, she found Rand asleep on the davenport. The Braille book he'd been reading lay twisted on the carpet where it had fallen. As Karen picked up the book and placed it on the end table, an encompassing warmth filled her. In sleep, the gaunt lines of fatigue in Rand's face were relaxed. She brought him a pillow and blanket and impulsively brushed her lips softly over his cheek.

Baking chocolate-chip cookies gave her an excuse to stay in the kitchen and have a full view of her husband. It was obvious he was exhausted, and she guarded his sleep jealously.

The phone rang, jerking her attention to the kitchen wall. Karen raced across the floor to answer it before a second ring could sound.

"Hello," she greeted softly.

"Let me speak to Rand." It was the brisk business voice of his associate.

"He's sleeping, Cora," Karen said with a glance toward Rand to be sure the phone hadn't awakened him. "Unless it's important, I'd hate to disturb him."

A heavy sigh followed. "No, it can wait."

"I'll tell him you phoned."

"Do that," Cora said sharply, then added. "By the way, I'm sorry to hear you won't be traveling with us next week." Her tone suggested just the opposite. "Rand said you're much too ill with morning sickness to travel. I've had my flight plans rearranged so Rand and I can fly together. You'll tell him that for me, won't you?"

"Yes…yes, I will." Confused and hurt, Karen could only make a feeble response. "I'll tell him you phoned. Goodbye." She heard the click as the other end of the line was disconnected.

She stood there, the phone still in her hand, staring at Rand while tears brimmed in her eyes. Rand knew how much she'd been looking forward to traveling with him. How much she'd been counting on this trip. He hadn't even bothered to inform her of his change of plans.

He was going to leave her behind, just walk out the door without her, without a word of explanation.

Replacing the receiver, Karen leaned her head back and closed her eyes. Instinctively, she wrapped her arms around her middle as a protective buffer to shield her unborn child. As if the baby could feel her hurt, her ache.

Perhaps she was being too optimistic regarding their marriage. Perhaps Rand would never accept her condition, never love or cherish their child. Perhaps he felt the necessity of being away from her to decide exactly what he wanted to do. Perhaps send her away. He had shouted for her to leave. Certainly the tension between them hadn't lessened.

Doubts, uncertainties, and questions pounded her from all sides, until her hands flew to her face as if to ward them off.

She needed to escape, too, but Rand had discounted any of her needs. He had been so angry with her because she'd hidden the pregnancy from him as long as she could. Yet he hadn't told her he'd changed their travel plans. Did that make him any less guilty? Rand had hoped to hurt her and had succeeded.

She waited until the cookies finished baking, then took a suitcase to the bedroom to pack her things. Where she'd go remained unclear—just away, she reasoned, to set order to her thoughts, decide what she wanted to do.

Carl was weeding the flower beds in the front of the house and glanced up when Karen quietly closed the front door. She jerked around when he spoke.

"Miss Karen, where are you going?" His eyes fell pointedly on the suitcase.

Karen looked away self-consciously, feeling like a cat burglar trapped in a bedroom. It was wrong to leave without saying a word. Everyone would worry, and she didn't want that.

"I'm not exactly sure where I'll go." Her eyes studied the tops of her shoes.

"Are you leaving Mr. Rand?"

"Oh, no," she denied instantly. "I just need to get away for a couple of days."

"Are you going to your family?"

"No." She couldn't put Judy and her dad in the middle of this. It would be unfair to all concerned; she hadn't even told her father she was pregnant yet. "I think I'll go down the Oregon coast. There was a little inn my parents loved, and they often vacationed there. It's someplace outside of Tillamook on the ocean. I think I'll head that way. Tell Rand where I am and not to worry. I'll be back in three days, four at the most. If you need to get ahold of me, Dad can tell you the name of the inn." She hesitated. "Take care of Rand for me, won't you, Carl?"

The older man gave her a toothy grin. "All right, Miss Karen, I will."

The drive down the rugged coastline was exhilarating, the scenery breathtakingly beautiful. Karen stopped at several scenic viewpoints to watch the waves explode against the huge, jagged rocks in majestic harmony. Several times she found herself wishing Rand was with her so she could describe the vivid colors and the brilliant beauty of the coast. Narrating a scene for him was one of the simple pleasures she enjoyed; it gave her a greater appreciation for the beauty of God's world. Rand had once told her after they'd made love that when he was holding her in his arms, it didn't matter that he couldn't see. For the first time in his life, he didn't hate being blind.

Now Karen wondered if he'd ever hold her again. The thought brought so much pain that she instantly rejected it.

The white shuttered inn her parents often visited was still there, but it was older and much smaller than Karen remembered. The family-owned enterprise had changed hands, but the new family was friendly and welcoming. Their teenage son carried Karen's lone suitcase upstairs, chatting the whole distance, offering advice about the best dinner spots, as it was nearing that time.

The room was small but adequate and had a panoramic view overlooking the ocean. Karen stood staring at it for a long time, watching the tide ebb away. The ocean mesmerized her; it was like watching sand sift through a bottle, wondering what would happen when all the sand was gone. The ocean was turbulent as the waves crashed along the beach, yet Karen found it soothing and relaxing after the long drive. She fell asleep without venturing from her room. She woke refreshed and hungry the next morning. In fact, she felt wonderful, better than any morning for three long months. A smile softened her mouth. Judy had claimed that if they were alike, the morning sickness would pass almost as quickly as it came—after about three months.

Karen was more like her sister than she realized. Anxious to enjoy the ocean air, Karen dressed in faded jeans, which fit snugly around her waist, and a pale purple short-sleeved sweatshirt.

"Good morning." She smiled at the boy who'd carried her suitcase the night before.

The returning smile was instantaneous. "Good morning."

"Want to recommend someplace for breakfast?"

It was the most enjoyable breakfast Karen had eaten in months. Without even a hint of morning upset, she took a long stroll along the undisturbed beach. It had rained during the night, hardening the sand, but as the sun appeared, drying the beach, it became impossible to walk in her tennis shoes. She paused long enough to remove them and flex her toes in the sand. She walked for so long that she lost sight of the inn. Her shoes were now used to store little treasures she discovered along the way, mostly small shells.

Pausing, she decided to rest before venturing back. The soft sand welcomed her weight, and she laid back, waving her arms to make a pattern of angel wings in the soft surface, then laughed at her childishness. How simple life would be if only she was a little girl again. Closing her eyes, she could almost hear her mother's worried voice telling her, "Karen, move back; the tide's coming in." But Karen had refused to leave her project, thinking her stubbornness would prevent the waters from sweeping away an afternoon's work.

"Matthew, do something. She'll be drenched," her mother had pleaded.

Helplessly, Karen had cried as her father had carried her onto the beach and she witnessed the sand castle washed away in minutes. Karen now felt much the same as she had then, the ache within her almost identical. That helpless feeling of holding on to something, then watching it disintegrate after having spent a part of herself in constructing it. Only this time it wasn't a simple sand castle; it was the love and marriage she had built with Rand.

Jerking herself upright, she brushed the sand from her pants. She'd come here to meditate, recollect her thoughts; now she found them too painful and forced them from her mind.

For all her wanderings along the beach and the unaccustomed exercise, sleep remained elusive that night. After fighting herself and her thoughts, Karen rose and dressed, slipping outside into the moonlight. It had rained again that afternoon, but the skies were clear now, alive with glittering jewels that seemed to smile down on her. The wind was strong as it whipped her hair across her face. It felt good and right to be exactly where she was and who she was.

Karen found herself talking to the child, her hand placed over her stomach as if to communicate her thoughts. The baby had barely begun to form within her, yet the overwhelming love Karen felt for this tiny being was beyond description. Recognizing and accepting this overpowering emotion had a very calming effect on her.

Never again would she apologize to Rand for this pregnancy. This child had been created in love, her love for Rand, if not his love for her. That didn't matter anymore. Releasing a sigh from deep within, she strolled back to the room and fell into a deep, restful sleep.

The next morning fell into the pattern of the day before. Karen walked along the beach, her bare feet leaving imprints in the wet sand. Today, she would settle, if only in her own mind, the problems that existed between her and Rand.

A conversation she'd had with Judy at the zoo played again in her mind.

"I think I'd die if Rand and I had to be separated for a year. I love him so much it almost frightens me; Rand has become my whole life."

Judy had laughed. The wise, knowing, older-sister look had come over her. "It's amazing the things a woman can endure when it's necessary. I didn't think I'd ever survive without Mike, but I have, and I will."

Recalling their conversation, Karen realized that although she deeply loved her husband, she could make a life for herself and their child without him.

Symbolically, she built another sand castle, far from the water's edge. It was hard work, carrying buckets of wet sand onto the beach, but now the tide wouldn't steal it away. Perspiration wetted her brow when she finished; a dull ache throbbed in the small of her back. She waited until the tide came in, proud that her castle stood serene and secure. Tears misted her eyes; she was ready to face what awaited her in Tacoma.

The drive home was made with a sense of impatience. Karen left early the next morning and didn't stop for either breakfast or lunch. The instinct of a migrating bird seemed to be driving her home.

Home, she sighed, turning into the long driveway five hours later. She'd lived in the apartment for a number of months, and it had never produced in her the feelings this long rambler did.

Everything looked so peaceful, calm. Nothing had changed, yet everything looked different. She parked around back and glanced at her garden on the way past. After three days without hoeing, it was difficult to distinguish between plant and weed. The kitchen door was unlocked, and with dauntless courage she walked inside.

Karen stifled a gasp at the mess that lay before her. Dirty dishes, food, and utensils littered the table, countertop, and sink. It resembled the kitchen after James and Carter had prepared a meal.

Clothes and books were carelessly tossed about the living room; the drapes were closed, blocking out the afternoon sunlight.

Karen put her suitcase down and immediately opened the drapes, stooping to pick up several items along the way. The house smelled strange, as if no one had opened the windows and allowed fresh air to circulate in days.

"Damn it, Carl, I said leave me alone." The angry words were shouted and cutting.

Karen paused as a dejected figure moved down the hall. The sight of Rand shocked Karen, and she stared at him with disbelieving eyes. It looked as though he hadn't shaved since she'd gone. His clothes were wrinkled as if he'd been sleeping in them; his hair was a mass of tangles.

"It isn't Carl," she said quietly.

A flicker of pain touched his face as he stopped. "Karen?" he questioned as if he wasn't sure of the sound of her voice.

"What's happened?" The whole house possessed a sense of unreality; Rand would never live in such disorganization. "Have you been ill?" she questioned, gazing at him anxiously.

"Karen, Karen." He repeated her name incredulously, his voice raw and barely above a whisper. "Where the hell did you go?" he demanded, his back stiffening, ramrod straight.

A bewildered frown narrowed her brow as she went to him. "Where have I been?" she asked. "I told Carl where I was going. You were asleep when I left. I didn't want to wake you. Carl was supposed to tell you."

"He didn't." Rand's smile was contemptuous. "I suppose he thought letting me suffer was poetic justice." His hand ran wearily over his face and eyes. "It doesn't matter." Slowly, he turned, retreating to his den. Halfway down the hall, he paused, his back facing her. "Why did you go?" It was as if the question had been wrenched from him, had cost him more than she would ever know.

"Cora must have tried again to reach you. I apologize for not giving you the message."

"Damn it, Karen," Rand bit out savagely. "You disappear for three days and apologize for not giving me a telephone message? I don't give a damn hell about Cora right now. I want to know why you found it so sam-hell important to run out on me?" His hands were clenched so tightly the knuckles appeared white. He turned around, his face twisted, like a man pushed beyond his limit.

Karen watched him with a sad, almost pleading expression. His agony...hers. "Cora phoned to say she's had her flight reservations changed, so she'll be traveling with you since…since I won't be going with you, after all."

Her response angered Rand all the more. "Do you mean to tell me this whole disappearing act of yours was nothing more than a fit of jealousy?" he questioned between clenched teeth.

"Apparently so," she told him flippantly. "If it's jealousy to have the man I married take two honeymoon trips with another woman, then that's what I am. I won't question if it's reasonable or unreasonable; it's just the way I happen to feel."

Rand swore harshly under his breath.

"Well, what did you expect?" Karen asked. "More important, when did you plan on telling me I wouldn't be going? At the airport? We're supposed to leave in three days. Excuse me," she corrected herself with a bitter smile. "*You're* leaving in three days."

"You couldn't come," he shouted, his face red and angry. Then he paused, taking several deep breaths as if to calm himself. Gesturing with his hand, he added with a helpless, frustrated note, "You're sick every morning."

"If you'd bothered to ask, you'd have learned most of the morning sickness has gone." She looked away guiltily. It had only been the last couple of mornings that she'd felt like her old self. "It doesn't matter." She felt tired and defeated. Holding a conversation while ten feet of hall separated them seemed utterly useless. She returned to the living room, stopping to pick up clothes along the way. She deposited the pile on the sofa.

"Did you want to come?" Rand asked quietly.

"Of course I did. You could have asked me, Rand."

She heard his uneven sigh. "The lines of communication weren't exactly open last week, and as far as I'm concerned, you're angry over nothing." His voice was raised as he fought for control.

"That's what the baby and I are to you...nothing," she intoned sadly, and turned to witness the hard mask that slipped over his face.

"I don't want that baby," Rand shouted.

"You didn't want a wife, either," she reminded him.

Rand bit off another caustic reply and paced the floor, saying nothing.

"It's obvious I expect more from your love than you're capable of giving. Somewhere along the road, I got the twisted notion love implies trust and faith. You've accused and doubted me twice." She took a shaky breath, gathering her resolve. "You once told me to get out, but you didn't say how far you wanted me to go. I think that time has come."

Rand's expression remained impassive and stoic. If it hadn't been for the nerve that jerked in his jaw, she wouldn't have known the effect of her demand.

When the telephone rang, she ignored it. "Undoubtedly, it's for you," she uttered sarcastically. "Probably Cora wanting to confirm your plans."

Rand jerked himself around and strode toward his den. The phone went silent. Either Rand had answered it, or the caller had hung up; Karen didn't know.

She drew in a deep, calming breath and leaned her head back to quell the emotion. She hadn't meant to say those things; her anger was hurting them both.

When Rand returned, his face was strangely troubled, the smoldering anger extinguished. "Karen, that was the hospital. Your father's had a massive heart attack. We must hurry."

Eleven

The blood drained from Karen's face, her hand flying to her mouth in shocked reaction. "Dear God, no," she gasped. "Rand, tell me he's all right, please."

"Carl's coming; we must hurry." Her husband's voice was tight with concern.

Later, Karen could hardly recall the tense drive to the hospital. She sat rigid with apprehension, her eyes closed. Matthew, her sweet, scheming, Scottish rogue of a father. Her lips moved in silent prayer, her spirit soothed by Rand's fingers tightly clenching hers, offering his support, his love.

Their shoes sounded loudly against the polished floors of the hospital as they hurried down the winding corridors.

Evan, Milly, and Judy were already there, sitting silent and frightened. It was as though they were in a stupor; no one reacted to Karen until Judy gave a feeble cry and stood.

"He's dying; surgery is his only chance."

Evan remained seated, his look despondent, his face buried in his hands. When Karen entered the waiting area, he raised his hopeless, weary eyes to hers.

Milly, tears glistening in her eyes, could offer no encouragement.

"What happened?" Karen asked as if searching for some plausible reason for such a thing to happen to her father.

"I've known about his heart condition for a year now," Evan answered her, "but I had no idea it was this serious."

"Dad knew he needed the surgery but refused," Judy added, shaking her head as if she couldn't comprehend what was happening around her. "He was waiting to die," she mumbled incredulously.

"To die?" Karen echoed her disbelief. She looked quizzically to Evan for an explanation.

The events of the evening were exacting their toll. Evan stared back, his face white and drawn. "I didn't know. I swear to God I would have forced him to have the surgery if I'd known."

Karen still didn't understand; her gaze moved to Milly, helplessly searching for answers.

"Matthew learned his heart was bad, but decided he'd rather die and be with Madeline than prolong his life. He told us tonight before the aid car arrived that it was all right now that you and Rand were married. He needn't worry about you anymore."

Her father's strange behavior this past year suddenly became clear. All the dates he'd begun arranging for her, the pressure for her to marry and produce grandchildren. His heart condition was the reason he'd coerced Rand into marrying her. Matthew had known she loved Rand, and when things didn't look as though they were going to work out between them, he took matters into his own hands.

No wonder Matthew had looked so wan and pale at times. She knew that he missed her mother, but not to the extent that he would rather die than go on living. How stupid she'd been. It was as if the weight of the whole world had come crashing down on her. She had been closest to her father; she should have guessed what was happening, should have recognized the symptoms. Her father had been biding his time all along, hoping she would marry, forcing men upon her so she would be secure before his heart gave out.

"We were playing chess," Evan began, interrupting Karen's thoughts. "He just fell over. I thought he was dead."

"The doctor says that unless Dad has the surgery, he won't last the night. They're prepping him now. It doesn't look good, not good at all." Judy's voice cracked on a sob.

For the first time, Rand spoke: "It seems to me the lot of you have given Matthew up for dead. Matthew McAlister is a cursed old bulldog; once he's faced death, I doubt that he'll go without a gallant fight."

The doctor appeared, his face grim. Matthew was ready for surgery. Again, the older man explained the procedure, making it sound very routine, yet didn't minimize the risks involved. Karen and Judy could see their father for only a few minutes.

The sight of tubes and IVs brought reality to the seriousness of Matthew's condition. Slow tears wound their way down Karen's cheeks and chin as she stooped to kiss Matthew's brow tenderly. Judy remained at the foot of the hospital bed, her hand over her mouth to hold back her distress.

Matthew's eyes flickered open; he appeared drugged and woozy. Nurses were keeping a constant watch on his vital signs and hovered around the bed.

"Dad," Karen whispered, leaning close to his ear. "The granddaughter you've been wanting so long is due in five short months. She'd very much like to know her grandfather. Please live, Dad. Fight this."

Gently, the arms of a nurse comforted Karen, pulling her back from the bed. "We're ready to take him to surgery," she whispered soothingly. "Don't worry, honey. We'll take good care of your father."

Judy collapsed into tears, returning to Evan and Milly, while Karen stood alone in the hall until her father had been wheeled from sight.

When Karen entered the waiting area, she'd never felt so alone or so afraid. As if by instinct, Rand met her, wrapping her tightly against him, lending her his strength, his faith. Karen clung to her husband, desperately needing his support.

The night seemed endless, each second, each minute interminable. The small group huddled together, as if their presence would aid Matthew's battle for life. By dawn, the thin thread of hope remained taut and capable of snapping at any time. Yet Matthew clung to it obstinately.

Sometime during the long night, each one fell victim to despair and discouragement. Only Rand remained confident during the endless vigil. His gentle assurance lent strength, encouragement, and hope; all four leaned heavily on him.

When Dr. Phillips reappeared, clothed in a green surgical gown, the family, watching his approach, remained paralyzed, afraid of what he would say, yet equally fearing the unknown.

Matthew had survived the surgery. He remained a critically ill man, and the next few days would hold the highest risk. Dr. Phillips advised them to go home and get some rest; there was nothing any of them could do to help Matthew's condition.

Rand, Milly, and Evan rose to leave, but Karen and Judy glanced at each other in unspoken agreement. They would stay, confident their love for Matthew was stronger than the power of death.

"Judy and I are staying," Karen told Rand.

"Karen," Rand coaxed softly, "come home. You won't be able to help your father any more here than you could at home. You need your rest. You'll only make yourself ill."

Stubbornly, Karen shook her head. "No," she whispered on a fervent note. "Judy and I are staying."

Rand didn't attempt to pressure her further. He left a few minutes later with the promise to return later that afternoon.

The hours merged together. Nothing mattered. There were no stars, no sun, no universe; nothing was of consequence while her father's life hung in a delicate balance.

The two sisters rarely spoke; the communication between them didn't require words.

The doctor had left word that Karen and Judy could visit Matthew for five minutes every hour, but only one at a time. When Karen went, she stroked his brow lovingly and murmured soothing phrases. Sometimes Matthew's eyes would drift open to gaze at her sightlessly, but his lashes lowered slowly, as if sleep had lured him back into her arms.

Seeing her father for only those few minutes wrenched at Karen's heart. He was so pitifully weak, so vulnerable. The picture of her physically strong, active father was far removed from the man who lay in the intensive care unit fighting for his life.

Rand returned and again attempted to persuade the women to go home and rest. Just as adamantly, Karen and Judy refused, fearing Matthew would wake, wanting them, believing with all their being they would instill in their father their own strength.

For a second time, Rand accepted their decision, remaining until late that night, having meals sent and ordering pillows and blankets when it became obvious neither of them would leave. Rand's quiet strength fueled Karen with desperately needed hope. She sat with his arms supporting her and relaxed for the first time in twenty-four hours. She was dimly aware of being lowered upon a soft cushion and covered with a blanket. A faint shadow stood above her, but the magnetic allure of sleep, sweet, blissful slumber, called, and she slipped into unconsciousness.

The next day followed the pattern of the first. Matthew's condition remained unchanged. Friends and relatives continued to visit, but there was no word, no hope to offer as Matthew clung to the delicate thread of life.

Rand was with them as much as possible, concerning himself with their basic needs of food and rest. He held Karen again until she fell asleep; she faintly recalled a caressing kiss on her cheek as she slipped into sleep on the third night of their vigil.

Early the next evening, the doctor appeared and for the first time greeted Karen and Judy with an encouraging smile.

"Your father has made definite improvement today. He's awake and already giving the nurses a bad time." He seemed to find amusement in this and chuckled over some private joke. "Although the immediate danger has passed, Matthew must remain in the coronary care unit for several days, depending on his progress. From there he'll be transferred to the progressive care unit." Dr. Phillips took care to explain the details of Matthew's recovery and left with an optimistic smile a few minutes later.

After the unbearable wait, the news of Matthew's improvement was like a refreshing, life-giving rain after a summer drought. Karen and Judy hugged each other, the tension broken as happy tears blurred their eyes.

When Judy gave a small, strangled sound, Karen looked up, confused and unsure, to find her sister hurrying down the corridor. Walking toward them was Rand and her brother-in-law, Mike Turner.

Judy floated into her husband's arms and was enfolded in an embrace that spoke of worry, concern, and months of longing.

"How...when?" She didn't seem capable of forming a complete sentence.

Mike laughed. "Rand contacted the air force, and I was given emergency leave. I can see I'm going to appreciate my new brother-in-law." His smile was broad; then he sobered as if remembering the reason for his being there. "How's Matt now?"

"Better, much better," Judy supplied the information. "The doctor was just here. There's a long uphill road to recovery for Dad, but Dr. Phillips feels optimistic."

Rand rested his hand lightly across Karen's shoulder, and she slipped her arm around his waist. The simple contact brought a ray of hope to the problems they had yet to face regarding her pregnancy. When she glanced at Rand, she found him smiling smugly.

"What did I tell you? I knew that crusty old devil was going to make it." His expression altered. "It's time to come home. Evan and Milly are coming later. They'll phone if there's any change."

After three restless nights, catching what sleep they could on a lumpy davenport, both daughters were ready to agree.

The two couples left the hospital, and for the first time in three days Karen breathed in fresh air and looked toward the sun. Her eyes were lambent, her relief almost translucent.

Carl greeted her with anxious eyes but relaxed after she gave him a reassuring smile. "I don't need to ask how your father's doing, Miss Karen," he said. "The smile on your face answers all doubts."

"Dad's better, much better. Thank you for your concern."

The older man looked pleased. "The missus has dinner waiting. She'll be glad to hear your father is improving."

Everyone was being so wonderful. Karen felt a knot building in her throat, never having realized before how the loving support of friends could mean so much.

"Thank her for me," Karen murmured, holding back the tears.

Home held the comfort of familiarity, and Karen looked around her as if seeing it with new eyes. Flowers decorated the table; her collection of figurines on the mahogany bookcase stared back at her, providing solace that would have been difficult to describe with words.

The aroma of the meal warming in the oven couldn't deter Karen from the thought of a hot shower and washing her hair. As she entered the bedroom, she halted in midstep; the open suitcase on the bed caused her to stop and stare.

"Oh, Rand, the trip...the lecture series. I'd forgotten. You were supposed to leave today," she said, horrified. Everything was so confused in her mind; time had lost meaning as the days blended together. The trip, their argument, seemed so far removed, so distant. Not since the phone call from the hospital had Rand's leaving with Cora crossed her mind.

"I'm flying out early tomorrow morning. There's no question of you accompanying me," he said flatly, pulling his tie free and unfastening the top buttons of his shirt.

Was he referring to the pregnancy or her father? Karen was too weary to question him.

"No, I suppose not," she mumbled, feeling dejected and sad. Rand was leaving with Cora, and all the things Karen had so desperately wanted to have clear between them remained to trouble her. All her efforts to normalize their relationship had been thwarted.

Rand was waiting for her in the living room, relaxing, his head leaning back against the chair, listening to the classical music they both enjoyed.

She sat opposite him, wishing he was on the davenport so she could be closer. "I want to thank you for all you did to help my family," she began, feeling awkward. "You were wonderful. None of us will ever forget it."

Rand frowned; his mouth twisted in a taut line as if her words had displeased him. "I didn't do anything anyone else wouldn't have done," he told her flatly.

Karen looked around her; the welcome of her home had faded from the lack of warmth in her husband.

Rand was leaving in the morning. Nothing had been settled between them, and already the cold mask was slipping over her husband's face. A knot tightened the tender muscles of her stomach.

"If you don't mind, I…I think I'll skip dinner and go to bed," she added, hoping to hide the despair in her voice.

Rand shrugged noncommittally. "As you wish."

Karen returned to the bedroom, feeling depressed and weary.

The gentle caress of Rand's mouth woke her the next morning. The alarm had rung, sounding as if it'd come from a far-off distance, but that had seemed so long ago. Karen welcomed the warm touch as he rolled her over, his mouth seeking hers. Automatically, her lips parted, savoring his ardent kiss. Her silken arms wound around his neck as his hand slipped under her nightgown, capturing the rounded fullness of her breast.

Karen gave a muted groan; Rand hadn't touched her like this since she'd told him about the baby. She was starving for his love and responded with all the hunger of weeks without him.

"I've got to go or miss the flight," he murmured low in her ear as his other hand stroked her exposed thigh.

"Can't you stay a bit longer?" she questioned, drugged with desire. Unfastening his suit coat, her arms circled the broad expanse of his back, stroking, caressing, drawing him to her.

Rand's mouth parted hers hungrily, and she clung to him, arching her back.

He groaned hoarsely. "I'll catch another flight."

Matthew was awake for Karen's visit later that morning. He was pale and so weak that his smile was no more than a slight quiver at the corners of his mouth. He struggled to speak, frustrated until he managed one word.

"Bairn?"

Karen flashed him a proud smile, her eyes sparkling with happiness as she nodded. "A granddaughter, we're hoping. Who told you?" He was unlikely to have remembered her frantic whisper that night.

Matthew rolled his head, indicating the nurse near his bed.

Mrs. Thomas looked away guiltily. "I hope you don't mind my telling him, dear. He needed a bit of good news."

Karen assured her it didn't matter; she'd liked Mrs. Thomas immediately. The kind eyes and reassuring manner had done much to relieve Judy and Karen during the bleakest hours.

"I hope this dirty old man isn't giving you problems," the nurse said with a wink as she connected another IV bottle to the stand above Matthew's head.

For an instant, angry fire sparked in her father's eyes, and Karen smiled at the sight, strangely comforted by this small display of anger.

Rand phoned that evening to assure Karen he'd caught his flight and had arrived in Chicago safely. He sounded relaxed and less tense than she could remember since finding out about the baby. It was a little thing that showed her Rand was beginning to come to terms with her pregnancy. Their conversation lasted only a few minutes, but when Karen replaced the phone, she closed her eyes, confident for the first time things would work out between them.

Matthew was much more alert the next two days as his strength gradually returned. Karen's visits remained short, and on several occasions she enjoyed the banter between her father and Mrs. Thomas. Their quick wits were well matched, and Matthew appeared to find solace from the tedious days in the good-humored teasing.

His first words to Karen the next morning were a plea for food. "Karen, lass, I'm starving to death. Will you see what you can do to get me off this sugar water and on to some real food?"

Even before Karen could assure him she would, Mrs. Thomas moved to his bedside.

"Feisty this morning, aren't you?" she said,

hands on her hips, her flashing blue eyes glaring at Matthew.

He lowered his brows disapprovingly. "How can a man be anything else when he's near fainting from hunger? If you were any kind of a nurse, you'd see about getting me some food."

"Listen here, you meager-witted, croaking toad. If you had any brains in that buffooned head of yours, you'd know none of the patients in the intensive care unit are allowed solid food. Be patient for once."

"Meager-witted toad, is it? Well, you're nothing more than a domineering battle-axe."

"Dad!" Karen's gaze bounced from one to the other. Mrs. Thomas's eyes were sparkling with delight; she loved this teasing raillery. Her father's mouth quivered with the effort to suppress a smile.

"Go tend your patients, nurse, but let it be known ye sorely task my temper."

"Thirty years of nursing and I've yet to meet a more ill-mannered, ill-tempered man." She continued to make busywork around Matthew's bed, and meeting Karen's eye, gave a girlish wink.

Karen's gaze followed the older woman as she moved around in the large, open area. Catherine Thomas's hair was completely white, and Karen guessed her age to be close to Matthew's. The woman's deep-blue eyes seemed to dance with mischief, and her smile was ready and warm. It was easy to picture this woman with her father; somehow it seemed right.

Rand telephoned from Kansas City the next evening and laughed as she related the scene between Matthew and Mrs. Thomas.

"It sounds to me like a little romance is brewing between those two."

"I was thinking the same thing myself," Karen confessed. "I've often wondered how I'd feel if Dad showed interest in another woman. I loved my mother so much, and Dad loving someone else is almost painful. But I like Catherine Thomas immensely. I wouldn't feel bad at all if they got to know each other better." The picture of the couple together brought a charmed smile to Karen's face. "What a pair they'd be. Mrs. Thomas is barely five feet tall, and Dad's well over six feet."

"Karen, I don't want you interfering with those two."

"Randall Prescott, I wouldn't!" She was surprised he would even make such a suggestion. Her back stiffened with resentment.

"Of all the couples in the world, you and I know what it's like to have someone intrude."

You and I, he'd said. Did Rand finally accept her innocence in the contrived marriage? So much had been said the night of her father's open-heart surgery to help her understand his strange behavior; Karen had wondered if Rand had understood the implications. Matthew was aware that Rand and Karen were in love, but he also knew his time was limited with a bad heart. Forcing the marriage had been a desperate act by a desperate man.

"Yes, I guess *we* do," she said evenly.

"How are you feeling?"

In the past, Karen had always responded with a flat "fine." Now that Rand possibly accepted that she hadn't tricked him the first time, maybe he would be willing to accept the truth about her pregnancy. Perhaps it was time to begin talking about the baby.

"I'm doing much better now that the morning sickness has passed."

"Good." The one word came out abrupt and clipped. They hadn't spoken about the pregnancy since the night of Matthew's heart attack. Rand's response didn't encourage her to continue, but she ignored the unspoken warning. "I've had to buy some new clothes," she added, forcing herself to sound bright and cheerful. "You'd hardly believe how rounded I've become since you left."

"I'm pleased you're feeling better." He didn't attempt to disguise his displeasure or the chill in his voice. "I'll phone tomorrow night. Good-bye."

"Good-bye." The line had already been disconnected; the buzz continued to drone for several moments before Karen replaced the receiver.

When Rand phoned again, they talked briefly, but he didn't inquire about her health. It was as though he were purposely avoiding the slightest reference to the baby.

Most of the discomforts of the early months of the pregnancy had passed, but her emotions remained sensitive and fragile. For several nights afterward, Karen had a difficult time sleeping, continuing to mull the problem in her mind.

It was a day for rejoicing when Matthew was transferred to the progressive care unit. His condition had improved so rapidly that even Dr. Phillips was surprised.

Catherine Thomas followed the small party down the corridor to the new ward, beaming a proud smile. Her delight at his improvement was apparent as she joked and laughed along the way.

Catherine stopped at the nurses' station and said, loud enough for Matthew to hear, "Keep your eyes on this ole buzzard, girls. He can be more trouble than a nursery full of newborn babies."

"Ha," Matthew emitted harshly, but his eyes followed Catherine without even a hint of anger.

Karen and Judy exchanged meaningful glances.

"How long before I get any decent food?" Matthew asked eagerly.

"Patience, my dear man, patience." Catherine grinned sheepishly at the girls on her way out the door.

"Dad"—Judy glanced out the window as if finding the street below an intriguing sight—"is there a Mr. Thomas?"

"Of course there's a Mr. Thomas," he boomed, his voice angry. "There must be a thousand Mr. Thomases in the world, but if ye're referring to Catherine, she's a widow."

Color rose in Judy's cheeks, but she managed a weak "Oh."

When Catherine reentered the room, Matthew's eyes widened appreciatively. His gaze fastened on the large serving of chocolate pudding. "Grand, pudding is one of my favorite—"

He didn't get to finish his thought. "But, Matt, this isn't pudding." She gave Judy and Karen a wicked smile. "This is strained liver."

A disgusted sound came from Matthew. "It

seems I'm beset by a cruel woman who delights in punishing a sick man." But his laughter joined theirs.

Rand had been away for almost two weeks, and Karen was miserable. She wasn't sleeping well; so much had been left unsaid between them. Karen discovered the pleasure she enjoyed in simple things diminishing because he wasn't there to share them with her. She worked in the garden, listened to mellow music, and eagerly awaited his daily phone calls. These were mostly a disappointment. Their conversations remained stilted and formal because neither would speak openly of what was uppermost in their minds.

With Rand gone, the baby was becoming more and more the focal point of Karen's world. The forming child moved often now; the first light fluttering, as delicate as a butterfly testing its wings, had confused Karen. She wasn't sure if it was something she ate or the baby. Gradually, the movements grew stronger, more pronounced, and Karen didn't doubt the source.

Rand phoned early one morning, early for Karen, midmorning for him in Cleveland. She was still in bed, her hands pressing against her abdomen, feeling the baby's movement.

"I know you don't want to hear this," she told him, her voice high with enthusiasm, "but I'm lying here feeling the baby kick. I mean a good solid kick."

"You're right. I don't want to hear it," he said dryly.

The balloon of happiness burst, leaving Karen speechless and unbelievably hurt. "Whether you face the fact or not"—her low voice wavered—"I'm going to have a child, your child. I did not create this child on my own. The baby is part you, part me. This should be one of the happiest times in our marriage, yet I'm afraid even to mention the baby. What am I supposed to do, Rand? What do you want from me?"

He sighed heavily. "I've told you repeatedly I don't want that baby," he said bitterly. "You seem to be living under the misconception that given time, my feelings will change. They won't. I'll have nothing to do with that baby. You've chosen to become pregnant against my wishes; as far as I'm concerned, the baby is yours, not mine. Don't expect me to touch it, hold it, or in any way have anything to do with it."

The baby was an *it* to Rand, a nonentity, unworthy of importance.

"Maybe you don't want me, either," she whispered through the agony.

"Maybe I don't," he returned.

His rejection knotted her stomach into a tight ball of pain. "That doesn't leave much to be said, does it?"

A long pause followed. "No, I guess it doesn't."

Fifteen minutes after the phone call, Karen remained in bed, the enormity of their conversation crushing against her heart like a huge boulder.

In effect, Rand was saying it was him or the baby. How could she possibly choose between the two? The image of a child the father refused to touch or acknowledge ripped at her soul. Loving them both so much would tear her in two. Rand was asking the impossible.

If this was the way he wanted things, forcing her to decide, then the decision would be an easy one. They had no marriage. Rand was selfish, hurtful, and totally unreasonable; he had been almost from the beginning of their marriage. They had made a mistake by not getting an annulment.

Karen jerked the suitcase from the closet and set it on the bed, throwing her clothes from the drawers into it without thought or organization. Her vision was blurred with unshed tears, her lips pressed tightly closed to restrain the sobs.

How naive she'd been to believe their love would conquer all their differences. Rand didn't need her; he'd just told her he didn't want her, either. Maybe it was time to prove she was perfectly capable of making a life without him.

She'd leave him this time, really leave him, not another three-day jaunt down the Oregon coast. A small, hurt laugh came from deep inside; three days without her and Rand had fallen apart. How did he expect to live without her, and for that matter, how would she ever make it without him?

She paused, sitting on the end of the bed, her tortured gaze moving around the room and sensing all the love represented there.

How could they ever settle anything when separated by hundreds of miles? Their telephone conversations frustrated them more than settled anything. They needed to sit across from each other and talk out their problems. Other than never being able to see the baby, Karen had no idea why Rand objected so violently to the child. There could be no more running, no more telephone conversations, when it was too easy simply to hang up the phone rather than talk things out. She needed to know his feelings, his thoughts; she needed to explain hers.

Tilting her head back, she closed her eyes as waves of depression rippled over her. Rand wasn't due home for another ten days. He was in Cleveland; she was in Tacoma. It couldn't wait;

they'd delayed discussing it for too long. She'd simply have to go to him...the sooner the better.

The flight touched down at nine o'clock Cleveland time. Karen was tired and hungry. The conviction she was doing the right thing was reinforced by every mile of the journey. As the hours passed, Karen recalled Rand's mother telling her she need only be patient. Rand would make a good father; would accept the child. Carl had told her that Rand would be handing out cigars, proud as any father. Karen need only believe this herself, trust in his love.

By the time she'd collected her luggage, gotten a taxi, and arrived at Rand's hotel, it was after ten. The clerk gave her Rand's room number and kindly offered to keep her suitcase, since she hadn't been able to locate him. Rand didn't respond to either the telephone call or the knock when they tried his room. Discouraged, Karen went into the restaurant for something to eat while she waited.

Where would he be this late? Cora hadn't answered her telephone, either. Were they together? With so many other things on her mind, Karen didn't want to think about Cora.

Seated in the dimly lit restaurant, Karen read over the menu. She hadn't eaten in hours, but nothing sounded appetizing. Where was Rand? She almost asked the question aloud.

As she laid the menu aside, the sound of a laugh, Cora's laugh, caught her attention from across the room. The lighting was low. At first, Karen was sure it wasn't them; it couldn't be. A bubble of hysteria rose in her throat. Rand and Cora were sitting together across the room, their heads close together like lovers sharing intimate secrets.

Numbly, she stood. Her heart hammered irrationally as she approached their table.

"Hello, Rand, Cora," she said in a complete monotone. A sick feeling rose in her throat as she saw Cora's hand holding Rand's.

"I'd advise you to remove your hand from my husband's, Cora. Otherwise, I'll have to create a scene in this very nice restaurant."

Twelve

"Please excuse us, Cora." Rand offered the other woman an apologetic smile and stood.

"You don't need to make apologies for me, Randall Prescott." Karen's gaze narrowed menacingly on Cora and was surprised by the lack of challenge. Was she so confident of her hold over Rand that she needn't show the least concern? Karen was studying the other woman so intently she didn't hear the parting words Cora issued Rand.

Rand held Karen's upper arm. "Thanks, we're going to need it."

Neither of them said a word until they entered the elevator.

"Let go of my arm," Karen demanded coldly.

Rand's mouth twisted, his look hard and resolute. "Like hell!" But his hold relaxed.

Karen didn't struggle; it would have been useless, anyway.

Once inside his room, Rand leaned against the closed door. "Just what kind of game are you playing?" he questioned, his voice hoarse.

Karen was trembling fiercely. She didn't trust her voice.

"Karen," he demanded again.

Turning her back to him, her arms cradled her chest to ward off the cold, the ache, the hurt. Tears coursed a haphazard route down her face, the strength of her will unable to abate their fall. Every breath became a sob, wrenched from her heart.

He clasped her shoulder to turn her toward him. "Karen, please don't cry," he pleaded.

Closing her eyes, she averted her face, burying her chin into her shoulder, her body shaking with uncontrollable sobs.

Rand brought her head against him, supplying the loving support she needed so desperately.

"I can't stand it when you cry," he said.

She gave a short, almost hysterical laugh. Almost from the time they'd met, all she'd done was cry. The power Rand had to hurt her was so sharp it was incomprehensible.

"Don't, please." Gently, his lips moved against her hair. His hands, which had been holding her, now began a caressing provocation over her shoulders, back, and hips.

His mouth sought the gentle curve of her neck. Just as powerful as his ability to hurt was his power to comfort, to love. His mouth found hers, claiming the trembling softness with a gentleness that caused her knees to quiver. His lips hardened in possession, and Karen could taste the salt from her tears on his mouth.

"No," she mumbled imploringly, breaking the contact and burying her face in his chest.

"Karen."

She could hear the rawness in his voice and knew he was as affected by their kissing as she. His chin moved against her hair as if he couldn't bear to release her from his arms.

"We need to talk." She was surprised by the strength in her voice.

"I know." His hold relaxed slightly, but she remained in the protective circle of his arms. "I've tried to contact you all day. Even Carl wouldn't answer. I've been sick with worry. I thought you'd left me for sure this time."

Lifting her face, she watched his reaction. "Would you care if I'd left you, really left you?"

Almost angrily, he broke the embrace and strode to the other side of the room, clenching his hands at his sides as he paced the floor. "Yes, I'd care." He ground out each word as if it were a weakness he was confessing. "I need you." He turned around, and his face shone with the intensity of his feelings.

"What about the baby?" she asked, her voice shaking violently.

Karen thought she glimpsed pain in his eyes. "I never wanted the child."

Her shoulders hunched forward in defeat until the baby kicked, almost as if the child were saying she must fight for her father's love. Approaching Rand, she took her husband's hand and placed it against the budding roundness of her abdomen. Rand resisted at first until he felt the activity. A sense of wonder came over his face, and for a second, Karen was sure she witnessed a flicker of pride move across it.

"That's the baby?" he asked incredulously. "He's so strong."

Karen smiled. Rand had referred to the baby as *he,* not as *it.*

"The doctor says I'm carrying the baby high; that's why I'm showing as much as I am."

Karen was sure he hadn't even heard her as his hand moved over her stomach in a gentle caress, his eyes proud but tortured.

"How can I be any kind of father?" The raw pain in his voice shocked Karen. "I'll never see this child. More than that, I'll never be the kind of father a child needs."

"Rand"—her voice shook with her own pain—"that's not true."

He emitted a dry, bitter laugh. "You know what's going to happen, don't you? It's inevitable. One day that child is going to be embarrassed to have me as his father. I'll never be able to do the things other fathers do." His voice trembled with emotion as he strode across the carpet like a man pushed to the limit. "I don't want that baby, Karen, but I'm trying. At least give me credit for that."

She watched him with a sense of unreality. "Rand?" She had once stood in his office reading over his accomplishments, with the realization that there wasn't anything this man couldn't do. He'd overcome obstacles and prejudices she could only imagine, but the thought of this new life they'd created frightened him beyond all else. "You're afraid, aren't you?"

He didn't bother to deny her accusation. "I'm scared to death," he bit out savagely, his face white and drawn.

"Rand…"

"No, let me finish. It's always been important to me to be completely independent. I've struggled for that. Now, within the space of a few short months, I find myself responsible not only for myself but first a wife and now a child."

"I entered your life with the subtlety of a racing locomotive, didn't I?" she asked with a tender smile.

His returning one appeared involuntary. "Now the baby is doing the same thing to the both of us."

Karen's smile relaxed, and she watched Rand with questioning eyes. "You believe me now, don't you? I didn't purposely get pregnant."

Rand's mouth thinned. "Yes, I realized that almost immediately, but I was confused and hurt. I lashed out in anger. I wanted you to suffer, and yet every time I purposely hurt you, I suffered, too. I created my own hell. Then you were gone for those three days, and I nearly went insane. I couldn't imagine what my life would be like without you now. Your love has affected every facet of my existence. I almost ruined what we have, didn't I?"

"No." Her voice wavered slightly, a lump of happiness choking off her words. "I could never leave you."

"Then, this morning, when I phoned and you started talking about the baby, I went cold inside. My stomach knotted into a ball of pain, and I knew I'd lost. I was going to love the baby. Perhaps I was even subconsciously happy you were pregnant. I got scared. All I could think of was all the things a father should do…things I'll never be able to do."

"But, Rand"—her hand gripped his arm—"don't you realize what you have to offer is far more valuable than shooting baskets or tossing a baseball? Why is it you feel that being a good father is synonymous with being a jock?" She sighed, her voice husky with emotion. "Just being the person you are is more important than any physical feat you could ever accomplish."

"But, Karen…"

"No, let me finish." She stopped to kiss his throat softly but found the temptation too strong; fearing it would lead to other things, she broke the contact. "I fell in love with you almost from the time we met. It didn't take me long to see past the angry facade you wore. I was sick with disappointment when I didn't hear from you after the Christmas party. I knew then that I'd never meet anyone who would be more of a man than you. When we started seeing each other on a regular basis, it was like every dream I'd ever hoped to fulfill." She gave a small, nervous laugh. "Every woman has a picture of what she'd like in the perfect man. Some see him as tall, dark, and handsome. You're all of those, but I've known lots of men who fit that description. It was your sensitivity, your intelligence, your strength, both physical and emotional, that attracted me. When you decided to break off our relationship, it was like dying. I knew that although someday I would probably love and marry another, I'd never love anyone as much as I loved you. It was a dreadful thing Dad did to us. Such trickery goes against everything I've ever known from my father. I understand why he did it now. But even before I knew his reasoning, I was glad he'd forced your hand."

Gathering her close in the haven of his arms, he gently parted her moist lips in a kiss that kindled a fire of warmth and need that quickly spread through her body. But Rand also showed restraint, as if what they must say to each other was more important than the desire between them.

"As much as I resented your father's interference in my life, I realize he acted in the only way he could. I would never have married you otherwise, for the same reasons I didn't want the baby. I left New York alone after the wedding with a harrowing ache eating at me. Your wedding ring was in my pocket, and every time I touched it, the ring felt like it had seared my skin. I kept remembering how you said you wanted a marriage that would last a lifetime and you weren't interested in a three-day weekend. You'd been so shocked, so genuinely surprised, when I told you about being forced into the marriage. It was like being pulled apart. I was caught in the middle of a tug-of-war between my intellect, my will, and my desire for you." He paused for a moment as if the memory continued to haunt him. "I wanted to hate you, make you suffer for all the agony I was enduring. At the same time, I desperately wanted to believe you. I yearned to hold my wife in my arms and love you as any husband. But most of all, I realized it didn't matter what you'd done or how deceitful you'd been. I couldn't deny myself any longer. I desired you as I've never wanted anything in my life. Do you remember when I replaced the wedding ring on your finger?"

Karen smiled softly. "I'm not likely to forget."

"Your wedding ring burned my pocket the whole trip. I couldn't keep myself from fingering it, as if touching it would ease the ache of not having you with me. I couldn't return to Tacoma fast enough to place it where it belonged. And then you weren't there."

"But I was," she reminded him mockingly. "When I hurried into the house, Cora had her arms wrapped around you."

"I could have choked her for that, but I'll explain the situation with Cora in a minute." Gently, his hand caressed her cheek. "I hurried back to put the ring on your finger. Suddenly, you were there, and I realized, ring or no ring, you were my wife."

"About Cora?" Karen questioned.

"Yes, Cora." Rand expelled his breath in a long, drawn-out sigh. "At one time, she may have harbored some hope of the two of us getting together. But she realized such expectations are useless. I'm very much in love with my beautiful wife."

Karen held herself stiff. "That wasn't exactly the impression I got tonight when I saw you in the restaurant."

Rand's returning grin was wry. "I've behaved like a madman most of the day. I tried repeatedly to get ahold of you and couldn't. I was positive I'd really done it this time. I'd lost you, driven you away. I booked a flight home for tomorrow morning. It was the soonest I could get out. Cora was, I guess you'd say, comforting me, assuring me that things would work out between you and me."

The unyielding stiffness ebbed from Karen. "From now on, if you need any comfort, come to me."

"Don't worry, honey. Cora knows where she stands."

Rand wasn't explaining the complete situation to her. A lot had been left unsaid, perhaps for the better. This was her husband; she trusted his judgment.

"And the baby?"

"My attitudes aren't going to change overnight. I'd rather you weren't pregnant. The thought of this child terrifies me more than anything I've ever faced. I'm trying to accept the fact we're going to have a family, but I'll need time."

Karen swallowed tightly. "I can't ask for anything more than that. The baby and I need you. We're willing to do whatever it takes, to wait as long as you need. Your daughter and I will simply have to learn to be patient."

Rand's arms tightened their grip around her, and he buried his face in her hair. "A daughter?" He looked surprised. "From the time you first told me you were pregnant, I've assumed the baby would be a boy."

"My dad has wanted a little granddaughter for years, and I've promised him a girl. Would you be unhappy with a daughter?" Karen questioned in afterthought.

"In truth, I'd rather you weren't pregnant at all. But as long as you and the baby are healthy, it doesn't matter what you have."

His words of indifference still had the power to hurt, but she disguised their effect. "Good, because I'm hoping for a girl." Unable to resist him much longer, she gave Rand a kiss.

Rand's laughter held a musical note. "I swear you're still more McAlister than Prescott."

With a warm smile, Karen cupped his face

and drew him down invitingly to her waiting lips. "I'm feeling very much like a Prescott right now."

Rand sucked in his breath and groaned before his mouth hungrily claimed hers.

Her response was automatic as she wrapped her arms around his waist and pressed her face to his shirt. Rand smoothed her hair; then his hands ran through it, tangling it between his fingers, and his mouth descended to the slim column of her throat. Nestled in the comfort of his arms, Karen yawned. Their emotional talk that morning, the hurried flight to Cleveland, the time difference between Cleveland and Tacoma, were all demanding their due, and before she could prevent another, she yawned again.

Rand sighed and gave a soft chuckle. "Come to bed, my love. You're exhausted."

"I am." Karen was too tired to argue.

They undressed, and a few minutes later, she was again securely settled in her husband's arms. A pang of hunger reminded her she'd hardly eaten all day.

"Rand," she whispered, "I'm starving—" She wasn't allowed to finish. Rand's mouth claimed hers again as his hands began a gentle exploration of her breasts.

"Me, too," he whispered huskily before claiming her mouth in a rousing, twisting kiss that left Karen weak with longing. This wasn't exactly what she had in mind, but she didn't bother to correct him.

When Karen and Rand returned to Tacoma almost two weeks later, Karen was amazed at the rate of Matthew's recovery. Although she'd spoken to him daily, she was unprepared for the healthy flush in his cheeks or the smile in his eyes. Karen was convinced Catherine was responsible for the renewed vitality.

"Karen, lass." Matthew flashed her a happy smile as they sauntered into the hospital room. "Rand, welcome. How was the trip?"

"Good," he responded simply, but the hand holding Karen's tightened. The trip had been the honeymoon they'd never had. It was a time of reassurances, settling doubts and misunderstandings, and days of wondering at the strength of their love for each other.

They rarely spoke of the baby. One morning, Karen had awakened to the feel of Rand's fingers traveling lightly over her abdomen in a gentle caress. They had both felt the baby's kick. Quickly, Rand jerked his hand away as though unprepared to touch this child or begin the simplest form of communication. Rand had told her he needed time; she must learn to be patient. Rushing things would do more harm than good.

"Dad, you look wonderful." Karen hugged him, her eyes aglow with a warm light. "Catherine," she greeted, and impulsively gave the older woman a hug. It was the first time Karen had seen the other woman out of a nurse's uniform and she was pleasantly surprised by her attractiveness.

"I should be going," Catherine offered, reaching for her purse. "Your family's here to visit now."

"I'd like you to stay." The unspoken message in his eyes was clear.

A smile widened Catherine's mouth, and she conceded.

"How are you feeling, lass?" Matthew's grin widened as his gaze rested on Karen's rounding stomach.

"Fine, Dad." She looked away self-consciously, praying he wouldn't go on about the baby in front of Rand. She wanted to warn him, plead with him to drop the subject, for she could already sense Rand's withdrawal.

"I guess I should have warned you, Rand. The McAlister women are a fertile group. I no more than hung my pants over the bed with Madeline and we had two girls before I knew what had happened. And as I recall, Judy had no trouble getting caught with James and Carter, either."

Karen stiffened, her smile frozen on taut lips.

"I could have done with a warning," Rand replied stiffly, but if Matthew noticed anything was wrong, he didn't show it, laughing off Rand's remark.

Karen continued her daily visits to the hospital, but as the days passed, Matthew's attitude became withdrawn. He was often melancholy, although he attempted a cheerful facade.

Several days later, Karen asked, "Where's Catherine? I haven't seen her in a while."

"She's busy, lass," he explained stiffly, "too busy for an old man."

"I know you asked me to stay out of this," Karen told Rand that night, "but I know something is wrong. Dad's miserable, and other than a few brief visits, I don't think Catherine's been to see him at all."

Rand's expression tightened. "Karen, your father is old enough to handle his own affairs. What's between him and Catherine is none of our business."

She gave him a determined glance. "I'm going to visit Catherine."

"Karen," Rand said with a note of warning.

"I'm only going to say hello," she assured him, her eyes glinting with mischief.

Forced to wait for several minutes, Karen sat in the waiting room that had been a prison of anxiety the first days following Matthew's surgery.

"Karen!" Catherine joined her; a smile of welcome didn't reach her eyes. "Your father's not worse, is he?" There was no disguising the note of anxiety in her voice.

"No, Dad's doing fine. How have you been? We've missed you. We *all* have." She hoped the inflection in her voice conveyed the message.

Catherine glanced nervously at her hands. "I've been busy."

"That's what Dad said."

Catherine avoided eye contact, her face slightly drawn.

"All right," Karen demanded, "what is it with you and Dad?"

"There's nothing between your father and me," Catherine responded tightly, and stood.

"Catherine!" Karen murmured in frustration.

With an exasperated sigh, she turned around. "You're more stubborn than your father. I don't know what's wrong, but every time I've been to see him lately, I get the impression he'd rather I didn't come anymore. I think it's obvious that he's recovering and doesn't want me around.

I'm nothing but a bossy old woman. I do wish him the best."

Karen watched Catherine return to her ward. What was wrong with her father? Why would he behave in such a way?

"I don't understand it, Rand," she told him later that evening. "Why would Dad act like that toward Catherine?"

Rand arched an exaggerated brow. "Karen, I want your promise you won't interfere in this. What goes on between Matthew and Catherine is none of your business."

"But, Rand—"

"No buts," he insisted. "Your father's behavior isn't so difficult to understand. He's going through a period of readjustment. He may love Catherine, but he wants to be sure he can offer her a healthy man. Let him work this out himself."

As the days progressed, Matthew showed renewed strength; his discharge date was set for the end of the week. When Rand and Karen visited the next night, they found Matthew out of bed, sitting in a chair waiting for them.

"Rand, Karen, I need to be talking to ye."

His tone was so serious, Karen wondered if the doctors had found a complication to his heart condition.

"Sit down," Matthew ordered.

Karen complied, her hand reaching for Rand's. She'd never seen her father act so nervously.

"Lass, I've already spoken to Judy and received her blessing; now I'm seeking yours. If ye have no objection, I plan on asking Catherine Thomas to be my wife. I love her," he told them simply, directly.

Karen could have cried with relief. "Dad, of course. I love her, too."

"Congratulations, Matthew," Rand added.

It wasn't until they were alone that Rand chided Karen affectionately. "Now, didn't I tell you things have a way of working out themselves without your meddling?"

Karen gave a happy laugh. "I knew you couldn't resist that, but I didn't know you were the kind of husband who would stoop to saying 'I told you so.'"

Rand's mouth twisted humorously. "Sure I am."

Matthew and Catherine were married at the end of October and left almost immediately afterward for a two-week honeymoon in Scotland and England.

Rand and Karen drove to the airport with them, excitedly waving them off. Rand was unusually quiet as Karen drove home.

Later, as Karen sat on top of their bed, brushing her hair before changing into her pajamas, Rand asked, "Now that all the rush has passed, how do you feel?"

She paused, her hands resting lightly on her stomach. "Tired." As the pregnancy had progressed, Karen had lost the ability to move gracefully. The baby's first gentle movements now resembled the activity of a soccer team.

"I don't want you driving the car any longer," Rand declared casually.

Her look was puzzled. "Why ever not?"

He walked away from her, hanging his clothes in the closet, as if reluctant to let her know his reasons. "Because."

A faint smile quivered at the corner of her mouth. "All right, if you insist." Rand was worried about her, about the baby, but was unwilling to admit as much.

"I do." His words were abrupt. "Either Carl will take you where you need to go, or if he can't, perhaps your sister"—he hesitated—"and, Karen, please wear your safety belt."

"I promise," she said gently.

Another month passed, the longest month of her life. Rand didn't mention the baby or her pregnancy. He touched her, held her in his arms, loved her with a tenderness that was beyond description, but he never spoke of the child. A hundred times, Karen wanted to cry out that her time was drawing near, that he'd have to hurry. She couldn't bear it if the baby was born and Rand refused to have anything to do with their baby or couldn't love him or her. Somehow Karen felt the infant would know, would sense Rand's reluctance, and the thought of that rejection brought a harrowing ache within her heart.

With only a couple of months remaining, Karen didn't think she could grow much larger. Even getting up from a sitting position proved to be a difficult task. Judy reminded her that large babies ran in the family and that James and Carter both weighed more than eight pounds at birth. But even she looked upon Karen with worried eyes.

Following her regular visit to the doctor in December, Karen sat in her living room with brooding thoughtfulness. As she stared into the distance, a lump began to form in her throat.

"Do you think Rand will be angry?" Judy sat opposite Karen; her eyes sparkled in excitement.

"Of course he's going to be angry. I suppose I shouldn't be so shocked, but how was I to know anything was unusual? I've never had a baby before."

Judy chuckled softly. "To be truthful, I suspected something. I could understand it when you looked down and couldn't see your shoes, but when you lost sight of the floor, I knew something was up."

Karen's voice wobbled uncontrollably. "How can you joke? Rand will be here in a few minutes. He didn't want one baby. How am I supposed to tell him it's a multiple birth?"

"You've really done it this time, little sister." Judy chuckled. "If I wasn't so delighted, I'd sympathize with you. But I think twins are wonderful."

The beginnings of a small smile formed. "I think I could be happy about it, too, if only I could be sure of Rand's reaction."

After Judy left, Karen entered the bedroom that had been transformed into a nursery. Running the tips of her fingers over the pink-and-blue-plaid wallpaper, she glanced around the room with mixed emotions. Rand had given her a free hand to do as she wished, never asking what she had done, not listening when she told him. She had tried to discuss names for the baby with him. Rand had cut her off, telling her she could choose any name she wanted. Little by little, she could see a softening in him, but it was so infinitesimal. How would he react to the news she was having twins?

The doctor had been so reassuring, so kind. When he had first suggested the ultrasound,

Karen had been surprised. The results confirmed his suspicions, and Karen didn't know if she should laugh or burst into tears. She chose the latter. Of course, the doctor had no way of knowing Rand's attitude regarding the pregnancy.

"Karen." The front door opened, and Rand called for her, his voice eager.

"I'm in here." She walked out to meet him.

"How did things go with the doctor today?" She stiffened slightly. "Fine."

Rand kissed her softly, his lips teasing hers, but his hold tightened as the possession of his mouth hardened.

"My childbirth classes begin next week. I can't wait any longer if I'm going to take them at all." Her eyes studied his face. "Will you come with me?"

His face darkened, and a scowl narrowed his eyes. "No, I'm not ready, Karen."

A lump of painful hoarseness tightened her throat. "That's okay. I understand." She broke from his embrace and moved into the kitchen. "I…I better start dinner."

Rand nodded, and Karen saw the flicker of sadness that passed over him.

Karen couldn't sleep that night. There didn't seem to be a comfortable position, and turning over was a difficult task. She lay on her back, staring at the ceiling in the moonlight, wondering how she could even broach the subject of a multiple birth when Rand couldn't accept or love even one child.

"Are you awake?" Rand whispered.

"I'm sorry. Am I keeping you up?"

"No." He rolled over, cradling her head on his shoulder. "I can't sleep, either." His fingers gently caressed the length of her arm. "I love you, Karen."

"I know," she whispered, the lump in her throat constricting.

"Honey, I'm trying as hard as I can. I know you're upset about me not attending those birth classes with you, but I can't force this. It's got to come naturally."

Rand believed the reason she had been so quiet and withdrawn that night was because of his reluctance regarding the classes. She hadn't the courage to tell him otherwise. Perhaps when he was more comfortable with her pregnancy, was closer to accepting the baby, then she'd tell him.

"Did you tell him?" Judy asked the next day.

Abjectly, Karen shook her head. "I couldn't."

"Honestly, Karen, when are you planning to tell the poor guy? On the delivery table?"

"If I have to. What do you suggest?" she questioned sharply. "He's trying to come to terms with his feelings for one child. I can't suddenly announce there's more."

"He's been so good to you."

"I know, Rand's been wonderful. But it's all me, not the baby."

"I don't understand."

Karen inhaled deeply. "He follows me around like a lost puppy. The other night, I found him standing outside the shower listening in case I fell. He calls two and three times a day and canceled his speaking engagements close to my due date. He's even hired Dorothy to do the housework for me. I'm barely allowed to lift a finger around my own home."

Judy chuckled, dimples forming in her pink cheeks. "It's a good thing. I don't imagine you're able to do much."

She laughed. "It takes me an hour to get dressed. I've only got a few weeks left before the baby comes. And as far as I can see, Rand's no closer to accepting this child than he was in the beginning."

"Chin up, kid. Things will work out," Judy spoke reassuringly.

The first glimmer of hope came a week after the break of the new year. Rand arrived home with a large box under his arm.

"Hi, honey. I'm home."

"I'm in the kitchen," she called, drying her

hands on a terry-cloth towel. Her back had been aching most of the day. Finally, in an effort to take her mind from the dull pain, she'd baked Rand's favorite cookies.

"What are you doing?"

"Dishes," she replied weakly. The ache seemed to be moving slowly from her back to her stomach.

He paused behind her, slipping his arms around her swollen stomach, caressing her roundness. "Leave them for Dorothy. I've got something for you—a present."

"For me?" She brightened, noticing the large box on the table for the first time.

"Go ahead; open it."

Lifting the lid, Karen stifled a cry, tears shimmering in her eyes. "Oh, Rand," she murmured tightly. "Oh, Rand." Inside the box, wrapped in tissue, lay a giant teddy bear. He had said the present was for her, but he had gotten it for the baby.

His hug was warm and gentle. "Hey, why the tears? If I'd known you were going to cry, I wouldn't have gotten it."

"I'm just so surprised," she said, sniffling, before he brought his mouth down to hers.

Sitting through dinner was an uncomfortable task. The pain in her back and abdomen seemed to grow more intense as the night progressed.

"Karen, are you feeling okay?" Rand asked as they got ready for bed.

Rubbing her hands over her stomach, she hesitated. "I don't know...I feel funny."

"Funny?" he straightened. "How do you mean 'funny'?"

"I've had a backache all day, and now it seems to be traveling around to my stomach. I think it might be a good idea if we started timing these pains."

The blood drained from his face. "Pain? You said you felt funny. You didn't say anything about pain."

Her hand traveled down his tense jaw. "Relax, Rand. I'm sure it must be false labor. It's almost three weeks too early."

"I'll call the doctor."

"Don't do that. It's much too soon even if this is the real thing."

An hour later, there could be no denying the pain that constricted her abdomen.

"I'm sorry, Rand, but I think we should call the doctor. This pain is too intense to be anything but real."

"Dear God." For a moment, Rand remained frozen, as if in his own silent terror. "You're sure?" he questioned.

Again, Karen was seized with another contraction, taking deep heaving breaths before she could respond. "Yes," she groaned softly, "the baby's coming."

"Carl." The name was wrenched from Rand as panic seemed to fill him. "I have to phone Carl...then the doctor."

"Honey, settle down. I'm all right; everything is fine." For the first time, Karen saw that Rand was troubled, unsure. "Rand...if you'd prefer it, I could go to the hospital alone."

"No." He nearly shouted the word. "I'd go insane sitting at home worrying about you. I want to be there when...the...our baby is born."

A minute later, Carl was knocking on the door, his face tight and anxious. "Miss Karen, are you okay?"

"It's too early," Rand repeated, as if hoping against hope she was teasing.

"It is too early," she agreed with a soft smile, "but I'm afraid no one bothered to tell the baby that."

"Oh, God."

The drive to the hospital was a bad dream. Rand kept telling her it was weeks too soon— she must be mistaken—and then shouting at Carl to hurry.

Karen was met at the hospital door by one of the nursing staff, who took her into the obstetrics ward. It was more than an hour later before she saw Rand.

He looked pale, drawn, his hair a mess, as if he'd jerked his hands through it several times.

"Karen." He caught her fingers, holding them tightly to his mouth.

She bit into her bottom lip to keep from groaning as she was wrenched by another pain. "Rand." Her hand smoothed his hair away from his face. "Listen, there's something I must tell you."

"No, you listen. I love you…I've done so little to deserve your love. The thought of my life without you is unbearable."

Tears blurred her eyes, and she drew a ragged breath. "Oh, Rand, I love you, too." Again, her stomach hardened and contracted. Against her will, she whimpered softly as the pain ebbed.

"Nurse," Rand cried, "my wife is in pain. Do something."

"Rand, you must listen to me…it's about the baby."

The white-capped nurse rushed into the room. "Mr. Prescott, there's nothing we can do now to ease your wife's discomfort. The doctor's on his way." The woman sounded so calm and sane against the frantic cries of her husband.

Karen smiled tenderly at this man she loved. "Rand"—she placed his hand on her stomach— "please listen, because I want to be the one to tell you." She paused as the grinding agony ripped through her once again.

"Tell me what?" he asked as she relaxed.

"Rand." She kept her eyes shut, afraid to look into his eyes, then couldn't help herself. "We're having twins."

"Twins," he bellowed, then repeated it incredulously. "Twins?" He shook his head as if stunned. "I should have known to expect something like this."

"Are you angry?"

"No," he denied instantly.

Again, Karen was gripped by the tormenting pain. Rand kissed her hand several times. "My love," he whispered as if the pain was his own, "let us work together to bring these new lives into the world. Show me what I can do to help you."

Her eyes shining with an infinite tenderness, Karen smiled softly.

Several hours later, after the delivery, Rand joined Karen in her hospital room. She was exhausted but radiant, content and happy as her husband sat beside her and kissed her.

"How are they?" she questioned softly.

A look came over him, unreadable at first, myriad emotions. There was pride, satisfaction, and a wealth of love. "They're perfect, Karen.

The nurses let me hold Jody and then Jenny. It was incredible to touch and feel our daughters. For the first time, I realize that you and I are bound together by far more than vows. The whole while you were in labor, I was experiencing this terrible guilt because I hadn't wanted a family. Then suddenly they were there, and I knew I would love these little girls beyond reason, as I love their mother."

Karen held his hand against her breast. "I love you."

"My wife, my lover, the mother of my children. You hold my life and everything important in the palm of your hand." Tenderly, he took her hand, lifted it to his lips, and very gently kissed her palm.

* * * * *